D1612638

WHEN TRUE LOVE WINS

Sonia Franklin goes to Bordeaux in France to be companion-cum-English tutor to seventeen-year-old Elise Blaise, who has been injured in a riding accident. When two handsome men enter Sonia's life, her heart is pulled in different directions. There is Elise's brother, Edouard, and their cousin, Paul, who both fall in love with Sonia. It takes several dramatic events to make Sonia realise which one is right for her.

KAREN ABBOTT

WHEN TRUE LOVE WINS

Complete and Unabridged

LINFORD
Leicester

First published in Great Britain in 2002

First Linford Edition
published 2004

British Library CIP Data

Abbott, Karen
When true love wins.—Large print ed.—
Linford romance library
1. Love stories
2. Large type books
I. Title
823.9'14 [F]

ISBN 1–84395–117–7

Published by
F. A. Thorpe (Publishing)
Anstey, Leicestershire

Set by Words & Graphics Ltd.
Anstey, Leicestershire
Printed and bound in Great Britain by
T. J. International Ltd., Padstow, Cornwall

This book is printed on acid-free paper

1

'Not here! What do you mean, it's not here?' Sonia Franklin exclaimed, hot, tired and, now, extremely annoyed.

The flight from Paris to Bordeaux had been fraught with mishaps. A supposedly missing passenger had been found in the wrong departure lounge but, by then, they had missed their flight slot. Another passenger then had a suspected heart attack and had to be taken off the plane, then unexpected turbulence had meant an uncomfortable, bumpy journey.

So, the crisp announcement that her luggage was not amongst that of the other passengers on her flight was met with uncharacteristic indignation.

'Will you please look again?' she insisted desperately.

Monsieur Blaise, her future employer,

had been very charming at her interview in Manchester three weeks earlier, and she had no doubt that he would lend a sympathetic ear to her list of problems but, even so, it was hardly the best way to start a new job.

He had wired her the times of her flights and informed her that she would be met at Bordeaux and driven the eighty kilometres or so north to the Blaise family residence and famous vineyard, situated between Saintes and Cognac. But if her chauffeur, whoever he might be, had left without her, she would be in an even worse predicament, since this was to be her first paid job since leaving university and she had less than one hundred francs in her purse. Not that she would willingly admit that to anyone. She would rather set off and walk the distance first!

However, it didn't give her much option to choose between a phone call or a taxi ride. For the moment, neither was amongst her first options. The baggage clerk shrugged his shoulders.

'I am sorry, mademoiselle. The only set of luggage left from your flight belongs to a Mr Samuel Franks. I believe he was removed from the flight shortly before take-off in Paris due to illness. Perhaps he has your luggage. The names are somewhat similar, do you not think?'

Sonia would have felt more lenient towards him if she hadn't been quite so agitated.

'No, I don't!' she snapped. 'I call it the height of carelessness!'

Suddenly thinking of the very short shorts and skimpy bikinis that were packed away inside her luggage, she added, 'I hope Mr Franks finds my luggage useful!'

The mental picture brought the glimmer of a smile to her face, restoring her more usual light-heartedness. Besides, it wasn't the baggage clerk's fault, so there was no point in taking her frustration out on him. She took a deep breath and let it out slowly, running her hand through her hair. It felt as though it were plastered to her head, reminding her once more of her predicament. She absently tucked a few stray strands behind her ears.

'Tell me what to do and where to go,' she said in resignation.

The sooner she got out of here the better. She was nearly melting with the heat and she just hoped and prayed that her transport was still around! She filled in the form that was pushed across the desk at her and bade the man au revoir, thankful that her French was as fluent as it was.

That was what had got her the job — an English girl with fluent French, to act as companion-cum-English tutor to a seventeen-year-old French girl, Elise Blaise, who had hurt her back and broken both her legs in a riding accident during the winter and needed intensive tutoring in the English language over the summer months, prior to going to follow her chosen language course at one of the French universities.

Sonia's small back-pack, containing

her purse, a packet of tissues, her passport and a small amount of make-up, was more ornamental than useful. It hung limply over her right shoulder as she made her way to the general waiting area. Her clothes were sticking uncomfortably to her body. She wished she had worn something long, loose and flowing, instead of the short and rather tight skirt that clung to her hips and seemed to be working its way up her body, and now she would have nothing to change into when she arrived at the Blaise residence. She groaned inwardly. What a start to her summer job!

Anxious about her transport from the airport, she looked around the building. It was almost deserted. There was a young family group awaiting collection, surrounded by what seemed to be an immense pile of different-sized bags — lucky them! An elderly couple followed a taxi driver out of the building, both dragging a wheeled trolley behind them, and a young woman was studying the electronic list of imminent arrivals.

Sonia pulled up sharply. It was possible that the young woman was the person who had been sent to meet her. Having missed her client from the previous flight, she was possibly intent on discovering how long she would have to wait until the next flight from Paris was due. Moving more confidently than she felt, Sonia approached the smartly-dressed woman.

'Excuse me, madame, I am expecting to be met here at the airport. You aren't, by any chance, my chauffeuse?' she asked in faultless French.

The woman drew herself up and looked disdainfully at Sonia.

'Indeed, I am not! Do I look like a chauffeuse?'

'Not especially. I'm sorry!'

She backed away, moving nearer to the exit, looking around for other possibilities. The heat was unbearable. A drink! That was what she needed! A long, cool drink of water! In her mind's eye, she imagined herself crawling over a sandy desert, her hand outstretched towards a glass of water that faded into a ripple of heat waves as she touched it. Her sense of humour surfaced and she chuckled as she rounded the corner of a drinks machine, colliding heavily with a man who, apparently, had the same idea as herself. He was dressed in motor-cycle leathers but she recognised him as a fellow passenger who had been quite chatty on the flight from Paris.

'Hi! You still here? I thought you would be well on your way by now,' he said in friendly tones. 'I've been changing my gear.'

Sonia took one of her precious French coins out of her purse and inserted it into the machine.

'So I see. Lucky you, having your own transport! My luggage has disappeared and there is no sign of my lift! Whoever it was has probably given up and gone.'

She opened the can of orange juice and drank deeply, appreciating its coolness. She wiped the back of her hand across her mouth.

'That's better!'

'Tough luck! Can I be of help at all? As I said earlier, I'm going to Rochefort, not exactly the same direction as you but . . . '

Sonia suddenly grabbed his arm.

'That's him!'

She pointed outside, where she could see a dark-haired man driving a bright red, sleek, open-top sports car past the building towards the exit roundabout.

'Quick! I must catch him!'

Thrusting her half-empty can of orange into the man's hand, she whirled away, darted through the doorway and out into the heat. It felt like running into a solid wall of fire. She raised both her arms and waved them wildly above her head.

'Hey! Come back! I'm here!'

To no avail! The sports car was fast disappearing from view. Disconsolate, her shoulders sagged and her arms fell to her sides.

'I've missed him! What now?'

She realised that the motor-cyclist had joined her, already looking uncomfortably hot in his leathers.

'You're sure that was your lift?'

'Yes. He's the man who interviewed me. I'd know him anywhere!'

She didn't add that he was so extremely good-looking, with a natural Gallic charm oozing out of him, that no woman between the ages of seventeen and forty would forget him in a hurry!

'Right! Come with me quickly! I've got a spare helmet strapped to my bike, but no leathers.'

He cast a glance over her skimpy outfit and grinned.

'I'll just have to drive carefully!'

'What d'you mean?'

'I'll give you a lift. We'll soon catch him up. Can you run in those?'

This time, it was her thin, strappy sandals he was eyeing dubiously!

'Just watch me!' Sonia answered with a wide grin.

She held on to his arm with one

hand, hopping precariously as she hooked off first one shoe, then the other, looping both sets of thin heel-straps over her fingers.

'Ouch! The ground's hot! Come on! Let's go!'

She grabbed hold of his nearest hand and they ran, laughing like children, to the undercover carpark, where he quickly located his motorbike.

'Name's Simon, by the way,' he said as he halted. 'Put your shoes back on and this!'

He handed her the spare helmet that he released from its elastic strap.

'Sonia Franklin,' she returned, swiftly fastening the buckles.

Simon was already astride the powerful machine.

'Hitch your skirt up,' he commanded, 'or you'll split the seams!'

Realising it was no time for modesty, Sonia obeyed and scrambled up behind him.

'Are you ready?'

'You bet!'

Simon eased the throttle and, with a surge of power, the machine leaped forward. Simon skilfully guided his bike on to the exit road and opened the throttle wide.

'We'll assume he's heading for the north circular route,' he shouted over his shoulder above the roar of his engine. 'If we catch him before or soon after Saintes, I won't have to go far out of my way.'

'Great!'

He obviously knew the roads better than she did, so she concentrated all her energies on keeping a good hold around Simon's waist. She didn't feel in the least bit scared, even though she knew they must be exceeding the speed limit. He rode steadily, dipping and weaving through the small amount of road traffic, in perfect control of his bike.

They didn't so much as catch sight of the red sports car on the ring road and Simon increased his speed as soon as they were on the auto-route. Sonia's hair was whipped by the wind where it streamed out behind her from under the helmet. She was thankful that they were moving fast. Her skirt was pulled high on her long, shapely legs and she preferred not to think about the view other drivers would have as they passed by.

They must have covered over forty kilometres when Simon half-turned his head.

'Is that him?' he yelled.

Sonia looked ahead. They were rapidly closing on a bright red open-top sports car. The driver looked perfectly relaxed as he cruised along, his dark hair barely ruffled by the wind. Sonia noticed that after a glance in his mirror, the man increased his speed. She suppressed a grin as he accelerated and they began to drop back. He obviously didn't like being overtaken, whether by car or by bike, and he would break the speed limit to prevent it.

Simon grinned, too, taking up the challenge of the race. Neck and neck they raced, Sonia's legs almost brushing the side of the car, so closely were they travelling. She tried to catch the driver's attention, hoping he would recognise her and pull over but he was too intent on holding his slight lead in this impromptu race to risk looking at the pillion passenger of his rival.

Simon managed to inch his way forward and Sonia took advantage of their brief lead to wave her right hand, hoping to flag him down. She was suddenly once more aware of the bareness of her legs and glanced sideways, meeting the driver's dark brown eyes with a sense of shock at the barely suppressed mixture of both admiration and scorn. She felt her cheeks burning and turned away her head, only now doubting the wisdom of their mad chase.

Simon edged his cycle slightly in front and, perfectly balanced, slowly waved his right arm up and down in a signal to the car driver to pull over and stop. At first, it seemed as though the driver intended to force his way forward again but something must have persuaded him that there was no threat intended and he gradually slowed his sped and pulled into the side.

Sonia hadn't planned what she would do or say. There hadn't been time. As it was, she hopped off the pillion seat, pulled down the hem of her skirt to a more decent height and swiftly unbuckled the strap of the crash helmet.

'Thanks, Simon. You've been a pal!'

She handed over the helmet.

'I don't suppose I'll ever be able to return the favour, but, who knows!'

'Glad to have been of help.'

Simon fastened the helmet to his pillion once more and raised his hand in farewell salute.

'Cheers!'

With a roar of power, he swung his machine back on to the roadway and he was gone. Sonia watched him go with a twinge of sadness. They would probably never meet again, just travellers on the road. But, he had gone out of his way to help her and she was grateful.

She swung around. The man in the sports car, her employer, Edouard Blaise, was staring at her coolly, his expression betraying none of the questions that must have been shooting around his brain. She smiled widely, remembering his easy charm.

'Bonjour, Monsieur Blaise! I'm here! Better late than never, eh?'

She held out her right hand towards him, thinking of how he had bowed over it, lightly brushing it with his lips as they had said farewell after her successful interview. His eyes had been dancing with his delight in life. But those eyes weren't dancing now. They were cold and empty. He ignored her hand, reaching instead for his gear lever, to put the car back into motion.

'I don't know who you are, or what your game is mademoiselle, but, whatever it is, I'm not playing!'

2

Sonia could feel the car begin to move. Her left hand was resting lightly on the top edge of the driver's low-slung door. She didn't have time to think about it. There was simply no way she was going to be abandoned miles from anywhere, in a worse predicament than before!

As she felt the initial slight movement under her fingers, she acted in the pure instinct of self-preservation, and flung herself headfirst into the space behind the driver's seat. She landed in a tumbled heap, all dignity forgotten as the car slewed round, its tyres scrunching in the gravel at the roadside. She heard a loud oath, which she didn't understand, her knowledge of French not being quite that advanced, as the driver once more applied his brakes. This time, he cut the engine and leaped out of the car, towering over her as she tried to scramble into a more dignified position.

'What on earth do you think you're playing at?' he yelled harshly.

Sonia managed to scramble into an upright position. She stood up, hands on her hips, facing him. This was ridiculous! How could he have forgotten her so completely? Without being proud, she knew she was attractive and could draw many an admiring glance from any male.

'Are you, or are you not, Monsieur Blaise?' she demanded heatedly. 'Monsieur Edouard Blaise, who, only three weeks ago, employed me to speak English with your sister, Elise?'

She was sure she saw a flicker of comprehension.

'No, I am not.'

She was so surprised by his answer that she nearly overbalanced. Her mouth fell open as she gaped at him.

'But you must be! You look so like him!'

She narrowed her eyes, taking in the

minute details of his face; the same olive skin; the dark brown eyes; the slightly long, narrow nose; the sensual lips; the same lean body, everything! He was! He had to be!

'Then who are you?' she challenged him. 'His twin brother?'

'No! But you're getting closer!'

For the first time the man allowed the glimmer of a smile to lighten his face, making him even more like the image in her memory. She began to relax. He was making fun of her, for some reason. As she watched, an eyebrow rose high, giving his face an enigmatic expression that both chilled and excited her. The man held out his hand towards her.

'Maybe we will be able to speak on better terms if you are not jumping up and down in the rear of my car,' he suggested.

She reached out to take hold of his hand but, instead, he grasped hold of her around her waist and lightly swung her out of the car, placing her on her feet in front of him.

'I am Monsieur Blaise,' he admitted with a barely distinguishable bow in her direction. 'Monsieur Paul Blaise, head of Blaise Enterprise. You have, no doubt, confused me with my cousin, Edouard. He did tell me something about employing a bi-lingual English girl to assist Elise in her language studies. He didn't say that you were also a circus performer who delights in doing crazy stunts between motorcycles and fast sports cars! So, what is all this about? Edouard may have employed you, but it is I who will be paying the bill!' he added, as she opened her mouth to explain, leaving her in no doubt that he could cancel her employment at any time.

She immediately closed her lips together, trying to quench the heated words she had been about to hurl at him. Instead, she made a quick assessment of his character and decided that a brief understatement would be the most likely appreciated. Accordingly, she simply catalogued the list of events leading up to the motorbike chase and her determination not to be left stranded on the roadside.

'A true maiden in distress,' he drawled.

'In dire need of a knight in shining armour!' she retaliated swiftly.

Paul Blaise laughed.

'All right! I believe your tale, though I would advise you against freely trusting young men like your dashing cavalier on two wheels and playing such foolhardy tactics on the auto-route. I trust that your judgment will be more circumspect when you are in charge of my young cousin.'

Again, he raised an eyebrow as he looked at her, making her feel more like a naughty schoolgirl than a mature adult soon to be in charge of a teenage girl.

'Of course! I was feeling pretty desperate when I saw you drive past the terminal. I just assumed you were there to meet me and had given up! Why were you there, if not to collect me?'

'Not that it is any of your business,' he said coolly, 'but I have been away on business for a few days, hence my lack of knowledge of your expected arrival. My cousin didn't share his plans with me. I wonder why. I think he likes to keep the pretty ladies to himself.'

'You both look very alike,' Sonia remarked, as if excusing the mistake she had made and turning aside the implied slur on Edouard's character.

'Our fathers were identical twins. My father was the elder.'

'Was?'

'He died before I was born, and my mother chose to follow him to the grave in preference to rearing me.'

He shrugged, as if regretting his impulse to confide.

'But, this is all in the past. We live for today.'

Whilst he was talking, Paul Blaise indicated that she get into the car. He made an elaborate show of holding open the low door for her, closing it smartly after she had seated herself.

'And you expect the return of your luggage when?' Paul enquired as he slipped easily into the driver's seat beside her.

The air of arrogance in his voice chilled her heart, making her feel both attracted and repelled at the same time. One thing was sure — there would be no playing about with this man! Realising that his question hung in the air between them, Sonia pulled her thoughts together.

'The baggage clerk said they would notify me as soon as possible. Tomorrow, he hoped. In the meantime, I must manage as best I can.'

His right eyebrow rose as he briefly regarded her appearance. They were back on the road and Paul's main attention was on his driving. She hoped that he hadn't noticed her cheeks as they flamed with colour once more. The countryside they were passing through was uniformly flat, but rows of tall trees rising from the acres of parched grass at their bases reached up to the cloudless sky, relieving the monotony. Fields of sunflowers looked ready to burst into flower and cream-washed buildings with terracotta tiled roofs and wooden-shuttered windows basked in the heat.

As they slowed down to sweep around the exit roundabout near Saintes Paul suddenly snapped, 'Get down! Slide down in your seat!'

Startled by the request, she obeyed his instruction.

Paul played a merry toot on his horn and Sonia could see that he had waved to somebody presumably going the other way. He was grinning widely when he spoke.

'You can get up now.'

'What was all that about?'

'Oh, just someone I know! Didn't want him asking awkward questions!'

Sonia was puzzled.

'What about? Me?'

He held her gaze for a second, then returned his eyes back to the road.

'It was a business trip I've just been on. Wouldn't want anyone to get the wrong idea, now, would I?'

'I don't know!'

Sonia's voice was sharp. She hadn't thought he was answerable to anyone, so why play games?

They had sped past the first signpost that named their destination and she began to look eagerly about her. It was rich agricultural territory. She caught glimpses of isolated, large manor houses, surrounded by clusters of low-built farm buildings. Most of the fields were filled with partly-grown corn. Many others, on both sides of the roads, were filled with narrow, shoulder-high hedges in regular, neat rows.

'What's growing there?' she asked.

'They are vines. This area is famous for its production of wine, most of which is distilled for use in the world-famous cognac. Didn't my cousin tell you? We are one of the main vine growers of the area. Although we bottle a proportion of our wines for our own use and for local sale, the greater proportion of our wine is distilled and sold on to the cognac houses. It is what has held our family together over the past generations. I have been negotiating some new wine deals whilst away. I don't see why the cognac houses should swallow most of our produce and market it under their name when we could sell more of it under our own label. It is a highly sought-after wine and I intend to make it even more so.'

Sonia was building up a picture of a hierarchal family system, of which Paul, presumably, was now the head.

'Do you live near Edouard's family?' she asked, wondering how closely she would be associated with her disturbing knight errant.

Paul laughed, but it carried a harshness that seemed out of place with the wide smile that now covered his dark-skinned face.

'You might say so. We all live cosily together in the family residence, my two cousins, Uncle Jerome and Aunt Veronique and myself.'

Sonia searched his face for the cause of the harsh sound but found nothing. She must have misinterpreted it.

'Does that work out all right?' she asked as casually as she could, trying to determine just what sort of set-up she had let herself into.

'It suffices. They all have a home, and I have a housekeeper and staff.'

'And if one of you marries?'

His eyebrow arched and Sonia wondered if she had over-reached herself.

'I'm sorry, that's none of my business,' she apologised quickly. 'I was just curious, that's all.'

Her voice tailed off and he replied.

'An interesting scenario, especially if both of us married! Just imagine, two wives at each other's throats! Maybe you are thinking of applying for the position. I wonder which one of us you would choose.'

They were now approaching a small

town. Paul turned towards the town square, parked the car and looked at his watch.

'Wait here!' he commanded.

Sonia watched as his lithe figure headed for the narrow street to their left and disappeared around the corner. She took a deep breath and considered the information Paul had passed on to her. She was getting the impression that it wasn't going to be quite the idyllic set-up that she had imagined. There seemed to be a whole host of tensions within the family, and that was from just Paul's point of view! What would she uncover when she met the rest of the family?

Paul returned, carrying a number of packages, which he tossed into the small area behind the two front seats. He smiled wryly as he re-seated himself.

'You are having second thoughts, yes?'

'No,' she lied, determined not to give up before she had even started.

'I'm sure everything will work out just fine.'

It was with some relief that they soon turned into a long driveway. On either side, as far as she could see, more rows of shoulder-high vines spread out. The drive turned left at the far end and a long, stone building came into view, its roof covered in the terracotta tiles so typical of the area.

Formal gardens were spread in front of it, edged in low shrubs and filled with hundreds of colourful flowers. Most of the exterior of the house was covered in vines and tall hollyhocks grew against them, their pink, red and white hues in brilliant contrast to the dark green background. Trees sur-rounded the building, shading it from most of the mid-afternoon glare of the sun. It was mostly single-storeyed but a portion in the middle had a second floor. A double set of stone steps led up to a stone balcony. Colourful flowers grew in pots on every step of the balustrade.

To one side of the double storey, a stone archway led through into what was obviously the private garden, separating the two portions of the building. An ornamental, wrought-iron gate filled the archway. Amidst the metal fleur-de-lys, Sonia could make out the lettering, **Domaine de Blaise.**

Paul continued past the building and turned right at the far end. Immediately, they were in a stone-cobbled courtyard. To the right, at the far end of the courtyard, were some large, stone buildings with blackened roofs. Nearer, over to their left, Sonia could see a number of garages and other outbuildings. Some were stables, their upper doors half open and a wooden hitch rail a few metres in front, with water-troughs hewn from solid pieces of stone. To her amazement, a peacock was strutting proudly along the ridge of the stable roof. Paul followed her glance.

'There are eight of them around somewhere,' he said.

'How lovely! I've never seen one so close to.'

'Just wait until they waken you in the morning! You might think otherwise then!'

Nearer to the house there was a covered, stone well, resplendent with bright red trailing geraniums and more tall hollyhocks were growing against the walls from even the smallest of cracks in the cobblestones.

As Paul parked the car, a youth came running out of one of the outbuildings. Paul was already opening her door and he tossed the keys to the youth, snapping something Sonia didn't quite catch. A horse whinnied somewhere and a murmur of voices came from a dark room. Paul followed her glance.

'The tackle-room,' he said. 'Do you ride?'

'A little.'

'Maybe you will do more whilst you are here.'

He took hold of her elbow and led her towards a stout, wooden door set in the main building.

'This way, mademoiselle.'

They stepped into a large, farmhouse kitchen. A well-scrubbed table stood in the centre, a platter of freshly-baked bread at one side beside a bowl of fresh fruit. Wooden chairs with attractive cushions tied to the backspindles were spaced around its perimeter. Strings of onions hung from the ceiling among smoke-blackened pots and bunches of dried herbs that Sonia didn't recognise. A large, black-leaded cooking range dominated the wall to the left. A wonderful aroma flowed from a large casserole on the top, making Sonia suddenly realise how long it was since she had last eaten.

Paul led the way through an inner door, into the cooler interior. She followed him along a short passage into a comfortable living-room. A woman, slightly older than Sonia's mother, was dozing in a deep-seated armchair and a thick-set man, seated opposite her, snuffled himself awake, his hands fumbling to grasp the newspaper that dangled from his lap.

'Uncle Jerome, may I present Mademoiselle Sonia Franklin?' Paul immediately introduced her.

Sonia moved across, her hand outstretched as Jerome struggled to his feet, and greeted her with the double-cheeked French kiss.

'Mademoiselle.'

'And Aunt Veronique.'

Sonia turned to see the now awake woman rising to greet her. She was a comfortable-looking, stocky woman, her earlier beauty still evident.

'Welcome, mademoiselle,' Veronique greeted her.

'And where is Elise?' Paul asked sharply.

An unidentified sound caused Sonia to turn back towards the door. A pretty but scowling teenage girl was framed in the open doorway, seated in a wheel-chair, which she had man-oeuvred awkwardly into the narrow space.

'I am here, but you needn't expect me to make her welcome. I told you. I don't want a teacher. She may as well go straight back to where she has come from!'

3

There was a moment of shocked silence, then the other three adults all began to remonstrate with the girl at once. In spite of the fact that Jerome and Veronique were her parents, Sonia noticed that it was Paul whose words had the most effect on Elise.

The girl's cheeks flamed and she muttered a resentful, 'I am sorry, mademoiselle,' before swinging her wheel-chair around and propelling herself away quickly.

Veronique made a move to follow her but Paul snapped, 'Leave her! You give in too readily to her. She might be an invalid but that is no excuse for bad manners!'

'But my poor baby! She suffers so much!'

'She must learn to overcome it! We all have battles to fight. If she will not try, then I wash my hands of her!'

Sonia felt embarrassed, being witness to a family disagreement so soon after her arrival. It was Jerome who noticed her discomfort.

'Please excuse us, mademoiselle,' he apologised. 'It is not easy to cope with Elise. Adolescents are hard work at the best of times. We do our best.'

Veronique hastily pulled a chair forward.

'Sit here, mademoiselle. I will bring you some fruit and a cool drink. Do you like fresh lemonade?'

'Yes, please. That would be lovely.'

'And then you must shower and change. Travelling is tiring in this hot weather. Where are your bags? Jerome will carry them upstairs for you.'

Sonia hastily explained about her missing luggage, drawing exclamations of consternation.

'It doesn't matter. A shower will be fine. I will rinse my things through later and I'm sure they'll be dry by morning.'

She was thankful to be shown to the

room that had been assigned to her. The wooden shutters were closed so the first thing she did was to open the windows and push back the shutters. Leaning out, she could see that her room overlooked the courtyard. It was in the shade at the moment, so she left the shutters and windows open and went for her shower.

On her return to her room, she was amazed to find some clothes lying on the bed. There were denim trousers and a short-sleeved blue T-shirt, dark red underwear and a matching dark red silk nightdress that brought a blush to her cheeks as she held it in front of her at the mirror. There was also a black fitted dress with shoe-string straps. A pair of cream canvas shoes lay on the floor.

She had no doubts as to who had bought them, when they had stopped briefly on their way here. Only one person had had the opportunity, but why had he bought them so secretively? Did he think she would have refused? To be fair, she realised that she probably would have refused but they solved her clothes problem, didn't they? It would be churlish to refuse to wear them. She dressed herself in the denim trousers and short-sleeved T-shirt, since it was still afternoon. They fitted her perfectly. Her long hair hung loose and damp but she knew it would dry quickly, so she simply ran her brush through it a few times to ease out the tangles.

Raised male voices were drifting up the stairs. Was Elise in more trouble? Sonia knew she would have to find a way to win the girl round if she were to make a success of her job, and although she realised it would not be straightforward living in this fractious household, she wanted to give it a good try.

As she went down the stairs, Jerome came out of the living-room and stood with his back to her, listening to the argument. She suddenly realised that the raised voices must be Paul and Edouard, and they were arguing over her — at least, over the non-collection of her from the airport. Really! What were they up to! She was here now. Surely that was what mattered!

She excused herself as she went past Jerome, determined to cool things between the two cousins, since it was she who was the cause of the argument. Jerome pulled at her arm.

'But, no, mademoiselle. Leave them. It will blow over.'

'It's all right, Jerome. I have two brothers at home who argue all the time. I'll sort them out!'

She omitted to say that her brothers were fourteen and sixteen, not grown men in their late twenties who ought to have more control over themselves. Jerome released her arm and she strode towards the room where the shouting still went on. She flung open the door, then stopped in her tracks. The two angry faces that swung in her direction were identical. She had absolutely no idea which was Paul and which was Edouard.

'Do you always behave like two

children?' she asked sharply. 'Everyone can hear you. Small wonder that Elise felt free to speak as she did!'

The man to her right looked slightly puzzled. He must be Edouard, she decided. The other man, Paul, took advantage of the lull.

'This has nothing to do with you, mademoiselle. It is between my cousin and myself.'

If she had stopped to think, his tone of voice might have deterred her from saying more, but she didn't pause at all.

'It has everything to do with me, monsieur, when I hear you shouting my name so loudly! So, no-one was there to meet me, but I am here now, so what does it matter?'

She turned to face Edouard.

'So, you had a wasted journey! It was unfortunate but it couldn't be helped. How could Paul have let you know that he had collected me? He didn't know himself before I landed on him!'

An irrepressible smile flitted across her face at the memory.

'Did he tell you how I chased him on a motorbike and hijacked him, thinking he was you?'

'No. He has been too busy telling me how to manage his estate during his many absences.'

Edouard's manner was not as relaxed and friendly as it had been at her interview.

'Did you catch up with him before or after Saintes?' he asked.

'Well . . . er . . . before. Why? Does it matter?'

'I didn't see you in his car, that's all. You must have enjoyed playing games at my expense!'

'You simply didn't see her!' Paul snapped. 'Don't make more of the incident than it was! How was I to know where you were going?'

'This has gone far enough!'

Sonia was feeling angry and a bit out of her depth, but there was no way she was going to stand by and listen any further. Something in her tone stopped the recriminations once more. She stood firmly, her knuckles resting on her hips, her chin jutting forward.

'If you were my brothers I would tell you to shake hands and make up, but that's far too mature an action for you two to contemplate!'

The two men appeared startled by her persistence. Taking advantage of the lull, she continued boldly.

'So, I suggest you agree to differ and separate at once! I mean it! You, that way!'

She pointed Edouard towards the open patio window. Both men glared at her but she refused to drop her glance. Suddenly, as a slow grin was appearing on Edouard's face, Paul laughed.

'Ha! A firebrand, eh?'

He stepped forward and tilted her chin up farther with the index finger of his left hand and searched deeply into her eyes.

'I would not allow many people to speak to me like that! And do not presume the same freedom again, Mademoiselle Franklin,' he said softly, adding, 'But, this time, I will do as you say.'

His eyes were mocking, sending a shiver down Sonia's spine.

'Wear your dress for dinner tonight,' he said softly, and without waiting for a reply, he turned and strode from the room without a backward glance, leaving Sonia shaking.

She wasn't entirely sure why. She laughed nervously, hoping her cheeks weren't as red as they felt, and turned to Edouard, wondering how much he had heard. Edouard merely raised his eyebrows and smiled. But Edouard's smile was more gentle. He held out his hand towards her.

'Mademoiselle Franklin, I must apologise for our behaviour. We weren't always that bad, at least, not too often! Welcome to our home. I'm sorry about the mix-up at the airport. The wife of one of our workers was suddenly taken ill and I drove him home and then went to pick up his children from school. I forgot the time. I'm sorry!'

His voice was sincere, and Sonia immediately relaxed.

'It's all right. These things happen. I was a bit fraught at the time but everything turned out well,' she replied.

'And have you met my sister, Elise?'

Sonia gave a small laugh.

'Briefly! I then went upstairs to have a shower. I'm looking forward to meeting her properly.'

'Good.'

He glanced towards the patio doors.

'I must get back to work, mademoiselle, and obey your orders!'

His eyes were twinkling and his smile warm.

'I will see you at dinner, at eight o'clock. Make yourself at home. Our house is yours whilst you are here.'

And then he, too, was gone. As Sonia took a deep breath, she heard a slight sound from the doorway behind her. She turned, and saw Elise there, her hands on the rims of the large wheels of her wheel-chair. Sonia smiled, ready to forget their earlier encounter, but Elise didn't respond.

'You have met my brother and my cousin, I see. They are both handsome, are they not? I wonder which of them you will like the best,' she said slyly. 'Edouard is easier, but Paul is more exciting, yes?'

'It's too soon to say,' Sonia replied, hoping her coolness of tone hid her turmoil of feelings. 'I'm sure they are both very nice.'

Elise laughed harshly.

'You think so? You will change your mind, I think.'

She turned her chair around, then said over her shoulder, 'You handled them well. You have my congratulations!'

Sonia felt that there was a grudging note of admiration in Elise's voice, but before she could follow it up, Elise had turned to go.

'Wait, Elise!'

Sonia followed the girl, catching her up as she turned into what was obviously Elise's ground-floor bedroom.

'We need to talk.'

'I do not see why,' Elise said coldly, propelling her wheel-chair forward.

'Well, I do!' Sonia exclaimed. 'I'm here to help you speak better English, and we can't do that if we don't talk!'

'My teacher tells me I speak the English very good!'

'Yes, you do, but not perfectly. Your phrases are stilted. You are still thinking in French and translating into English as you speak.'

'My English is as good as your French!'

Sonia laughed.

'Maybe, but I know my French could be better. I am hoping to improve it whilst I am here.'

'So, we will speak French together!'

A glimmer of a smile hovered for a moment or two on Elise's face. Sonia seized the opportunity for an answering smile

'Not so fast! You and I will speak English. I will speak French with your family. What have you to lose?'

Elise slowly turned her chair around to face Sonia. She looked so unhappy that Sonia felt a surge of pity for the girl, but tried not to show it. Elise, nonetheless, detected her sympathy.

'I have not the need for a nursemaid.'

'Who said anything about being a nursemaid? You seem to manage pretty well as you are. I am only four years older than you. I'm not a nurse.'

'Well, I will think about it.'

She silently swung her wheel-chair around and went into her room. Sonia let her go, feeling she had made a start in winning Elise around. She then joined Veronique in the kitchen, where preparations were being made for the evening meal. They spent a pleasant hour exchanging family histories until Veronique sent her upstairs to change for dinner.

'Will your clothes be dry?' Veronique asked anxiously.

Sonia felt reluctant to tell her about the dress Paul had bought for her but knew there was no way she could avoid it. Better here than in front of everyone at dinner! If Veronique was surprised, she didn't say so.

'He can afford it,' she commented.

Her voice was low and Sonia wasn't sure if there was a trace of bitterness in it. Deciding that she had a lot to learn abut this family, Sonia went upstairs.

The dress looked stunning on her. She didn't often wear black, more from a fear of it being too sombre a colour for her but she now realised that that fear was unnecessary. If she had had a choice of what to wear, she might have thought it was too formal for family dinner but, since she had no choice, the decision was already made. Paul had accurately guessed her size and, as predicted, the dress fitted perfectly.

She decided to wear her hair up and she fastened it loosely on top of her head, leaving a few tendrils curling in front of her ears. She had put her few items of jewellery into her main luggage so she had nothing with which to complement the dress.

Her strappy sandals were fairly new and didn't look too out of place. With a last look in the mirror, she took a deep breath and left her room. As she turned the corner of the stairs, she realised that either Paul or Edouard had preceded her down. She couldn't be sure who it was from behind. He sensed her presence behind him and turned round. The look of blatant admiration made her catch her breath. It took all of her self-control to enable her to continue calmly down the stairs. She smiled.

'Thank you for the clothes, Paul, though I'm sure your family would have forgiven my lack of correct attire until my luggage returns. This dress is . . . '

' . . . superb!' a voice behind her exclaimed, completing her sentence.

She whirled around. The other one was there. She looked from one to the other, once again unsure of their identity. It was Edouard, in front of her, who ended her dilemma.

'Paul is correct. You look superb, mademoiselle! I regret that your thanks to me are misplaced, but my admiration is sincere, I assure you. You will grace our dinner table!'

Paul tripped lightly down the last few stairs, impeccably dressed in a dark lounge suit. He was smiling widely, pleased with the effect of his gift. As Sonia hesitated between the two of them, still nonplussed by her mistake, Paul stood behind her.

'The dress on its own is beautiful, Mademoiselle Sonia, but, on you it is stunning. May I add my compliments to those of my cousin?'

Sonia turned round to find his eyes, not on her, but sending a look of mocking triumph over her shoulder towards Edouard. She stepped away sharply.

'Thank you, and thank you for the clothes. I'm sure they were quite unnecessary but it was kind of you to think of it. You must stop the appropriate amount out of my salary.'

Paul raised his eyebrows.

'Think of them as a gift from the

family. As you see, we dress for dinner. I didn't want you to feel in any way inappropriately attired.'

Jerome was approaching them suitably dressed and Elise propelled herself forward, wearing a simple, fitted sundress. Jerome seemed oblivious to the tension but Elise grinned wickedly as she directed her wheel-chair straight at the group. It was Edouard who adroitly pulled Sonia to his side as Paul stepped forward, grabbed the handles of the wheel-chair and swivelled it around.

'Road hog!' he teased.

'Tom cats!' Elise chortled, unabashed by Paul's sharp reprimand.

She made a great show of appraising Sonia's dress.

'Very nice!'

It was after ten when coffee was eventually served after a lovely meal and, as soon as was politely possible, Sonia excused herself and bade everyone good-night. It had been a long day and she was tired. After a quick shower, she slipped into bed but sleep wouldn't come. Events of the day imprinted themselves in her mind in chaotic order.

Just as she felt drowsy enough to drift off to sleep, she was suddenly wide awake again. A memory of Paul telling her to slide down in her seat in his car at the roundabout at Saintes vividly replayed in her mind.

It must have been Edouard who was in the other car! Sonia felt bewildered. Paul had deliberately let Edouard make an unnecessary journey. Why had he done that? And how childish! She, for one, was not impressed!

4

The raucous call that awakened her in the morning drew her out of bed. She flung wide open the window and shutters. The sun was already shining brilliantly and the beautiful peacock responsible for the early-morning call was perched proudly on top of the steeply-roofed cover of the stone well, his blue feathers glistening in the sunshine, long tail trailing majestically behind.

Sonia laughed in delight. She breathed in the fresh, morning air, feeling enthusiastic about her first full day at her new job. The disagreements of the previous evening had dimmed in her memory and the sunshine seemed to fill the day with promise. Only Edouard was breakfasting in the kitchen when she entered. He greeted her with a bright smile.

'Bonjour, Sonia. You slept well?'

'Yes, thank you. I wasn't sure what time to get up. What time does Elise usually start the day?'

'Usually after nine. Maman takes her breakfast to her, then helps her to get showered and dressed. That's probably where she is now. Breakfast is always an informal meal so help yourself to croissants or rolls.'

He nodded towards the coffee pot on the edge of the stove.

'I have just made a fresh pot of coffee. What do you intend to do today?'

Sonia picked up a freshly-baked roll and split it open.

'I want to get to know Elise a lot better. The better friends we are, the better she will learn to speak fluent English with me. What do you suggest?'

'I am inspecting the vines this morning. The ground is too uneven for Elise's wheel-chair but, if you suggest she shows you around the farm, I should be free to take you around our pressing area and the cellars by about eleven o'clock. Would you like that?'

'Yes, indeed I would! I really don't know very much about wine-making, only the drinking of it!'

'That's a good place to start! The tasting is essential to the final production.'

They could hear Elise approaching. Edouard raised his eyebrows as her grumbling tones preceded her.

'How can you expect me to live what you call a normal life if you constantly oversleep, Maman? You know very well that I can't get myself washed and dressed on my own! Now we will be rushing all day!'

'I didn't do it on purpose, Elise. I just haven't been sleeping very well lately, and you don't make it any easier for me, with all your tantrums! All we want is for you to get well and be ready to take your place at university in October.'

Veronique struggled to get the wheelchair through the doorway. Edouard rushed forward to help her, looking at her in concern.

'Are you feeling unwell, Maman? What is the matter?'

'Oh, I don't know. I just feel a bit under the weather. I haven't been sleeping properly for a few weeks. I'm probably worrying about Elise.'

Elise immediately looked contrite.

'I'm sorry, Maman. I haven't meant to worry you. I will try to be more friendly.'

She looked at Sonia, somewhat shamefaced.

'I'm sorry, mademoiselle. I didn't mean to be bad-mannered.'

Sonia smiled at her.

'That's all right, Elise. I do understand. And please, call me Sonia. I want us to be friends, then I can help you.'

'We were just saying that it would be a good idea if you took Sonia to look around the farm this morning,' Edouard told Elise. 'How about it?'

'I suppose so,' she agreed somewhat

grudgingly, casting Edouard a suspicious look. 'I won't . . . you know.'

'I know, I know. It's all right! Just do what you can.'

'Well, as long as that's understood!'

She turned to Sonia.

'Just give me time to have something to eat. Is that all right, Maman? Can you manage on your own this morning?'

'Yes, yes. You go out. It will do you good. I'll manage. Haven't I always managed?'

Veronique made a show of bustling about the kitchen. Sonia felt a bit concerned but was unable to judge just how much under the weather Veronique might be. Both Edouard and Elise now seemed to have been convinced that it was nothing serious, so she accepted their judgement. Her main thought was that Elise had decided to accept her a little more readily, which could only be good.

Once on their way outside, Sonia could tell Elise was really trying to make up for her behaviour of the previous day and she followed her around, keenly interested in discovering what her temporary home was like. She discovered that many of the outbuildings were used as storehouses for the farm equipment, much of it state-of-the-art, modern machinery that, somehow, she hadn't expected, especially the large vine-stripping machine. It didn't fit in with her romantic notion of fields full of local peasants filling hoppers on their backs.

'That is because, when the grapes are ready to be gathered, they need to be gathered quickly,' Elise explained. 'Otherwise, they are too ripe, too sweet, and then they are wasted.'

'I thought the grapes had to be sweet to make a good wine.'

'Not when the grape juice has to be distilled to make into cognac. It needs to be, acid, do you say?'

'Yes, or sharp.'

'We used to employ many workers at harvest time, but we cannot always get them now. Not at such short notice, and when Edouard knows the grapes are ready, they have to be gathered that day.'

The tackle room was empty when they reached it. The smell of leather filled the air. Sonia noticed that Elise's face had tensed. She manoeuvred her wheel-chair so that Sonia could pass in front of her but made no move to follow her in.

'Each horse has its own set of tackle,' Elise explained from the doorway. 'The riding hats are kept in there as well. If you ride, you will find one to fit.'

She spoke in tight sentences, her face turned away. Sonia glanced around the room but made no comment. It must be difficult for Elise to come face to face with the familiar objects that were part of the incident that deprived her of her ability to walk. She would have to keep that in mind.

They moved on to the stables. Sonia was beginning to wonder if this was such a good idea but Elise propelled her wheel-chair towards them. Her mouth was set in a determined line and her eyes were cold and hard.

'Let's go back to the house, Elise,' Sonia suggested. 'I can see the horses some other time.'

'The horses are not here,' Elise said, her voice empty of all emotion. 'They are in the fields.'

'Then let's go back.'

'No. I have to face this. Paul is forever telling me that I must.'

Elise's face was white and pinched. Her inner struggle was showing through. Sonia felt at a loss what to do.

'Have you not been in the stables since your accident?'

'No.'

'You don't have to do it today.'

Elise bit her lower lip, undecided what to do.

'I tell you what,' Sonia suggested. 'Why don't you go and ask your mother to put the coffee pot on and I'll take a quick look in here by myself?'

She reached down and turned Elise's

chair around, giving her a small push back towards the house. To her relief, Elise did as she was told. It was obvious that she was not ready to take that step and she didn't want to be the one to push her beyond her limit.

She quickly made a tour, noting a horse's name above all but one of the inner stable doors. Was that the one that had thrown Elise? Had the animal been put down? No wonder she didn't want to come in. She looked around. The stables were clean and strewn with fresh hay. A glance at her watch told her it was time to return to the house.

Edouard joined her on her way, falling into step beside her.

'How did you get on with Elise?'

'Fine. I sent her back to the house to make sure the coffee was ready. I'm thirsty. It is so hot here!'

She didn't want to risk betraying Elise's slender confidence in her by speaking of her reluctance to enter the stable, and Edouard didn't pursue the question. He nodded, pursing his lips thoughtfully.

'Are you ready to inspect our wine press later?'

'Yes, as long as Elise doesn't need me. You know, I don't feel as though I am earning my wage. You will tell me if you think I should be doing more, won't you?'

'We will go when Elise's physiotherapist is here. She comes each day, usually just after lunch, but she is coming early today. I'll take you after coffee. To be quite honest, I think Elise needs you more than just as a language tutor. I interviewed over half a dozen young ladies the other week. You stood out as being someone with whom I felt Elise would feel an affinity. Her accident damaged more than her body. Her body is healing but she doesn't seem ready to accept it. Can you understand that?'

Sonia hesitated, hoping he wasn't expecting her to have much medical knowledge.

'I can accept it, but I don't really understand the psychology behind it. I believe our physical well-being is tied closely with our mental, emotional and even our spiritual well-being. When one is damaged, the others can be thrown out of harmony. If it's any help to you, I like Elise. I sense a deep distress in her and I just hope I can help her.'

Edouard laid a hand across her shoulders as they paused outside the kitchen door, giving them a gentle squeeze.

'I think you will, but don't expect to do it overnight. Give yourself time to build up a friendship.'

'How very cosy!'

Sonia and Edouard turned round at the unexpected interruption to see Paul approaching behind them.

'Has Elise been outside today?' he asked directly of Sonia.

'Yes. She took me on a tour of the farm and stables.'

Sonia felt flustered, wondering what lay behind his question. Didn't Elise go out much? No-one had said.

'Good!' he said, sounding surprised. 'She has decided to stop her silly charade, has she? You are obviously good for her. Congratulations.'

Sonia exchanged a swift glance with Edouard, aware that Paul had read more into her reply than she had meant. But, if she corrected him, she would be announcing Elise's failure and she didn't want to do that.

'We are going in for a cup of coffee,' she said instead, adding, 'Elise has just gone ahead of us.'

'Then I will join you, as long as my cousin doesn't object.'

Paul raised his eyebrow, waiting for a response from Edouard. Edouard had opened the door and now he gently ushered Sonia into the house ahead of him.

'Not at all,' he said over his shoulder. 'You're the boss, after all.'

Paul merely grinned at the reply, as he followed them inside.

Elise was polishing a lapful of cutlery,

chatting to her mother, looking happier than Sonia had seen her so far.

'Hello, Paul. Corrine has been on the phone for you. She couldn't get through on your mobile. She said to ring her back when you have time.'

'Right! And what's this I hear? Sonia told me about you taking her to see the stables. Changed your mind, huh?'

Elise's face went white, then she coloured vividly.

'How could you?' she cried at Sonia.

She threw the cutlery on to the floor and swiftly propelled her wheel-chair out of the kitchen.

'Elise! Don't go!'

With a horrified look at Edouard, Sonia ran after Elise. When she reached the passageway, she was in time to hear the door to Elise's bedroom slam shut. She hurried down the passage.

'Elise! Open the door! Let me explain! I didn't tell Paul. Honestly!'

'Go away! I do not want to see you, ever!'

'Oh, Elise. I'm sorry, honestly. He

misunderstood something I said. I didn't tell him anything!'

She waited for a response but none came.

'Elise!'

When no answer came, her shoulders sagged. She looked helplessly at the closed door. Just when she thought she had been making headway, too! When she returned to the kitchen only Paul and Veronique were there.

'What was all that about?' Paul asked, pouring himself a cup of coffee. 'Want one?'

'Yes, please. Er, it's just that you jumped to the wrong conclusion. Elise took me to see the stables, but she didn't take me inside. She doesn't feel ready for that yet.'

'Nonsense! She's just playing to her audience! It's time she got her act together. She is testing you. She is used to having too much of her own way and is finding out how far she can push you. You will have to be firm with her or she will lead you a dance, mademoiselle, like she does with her mother, isn't that so, Aunt Veronique?'

Veronique shook her head and turned away.

'She needs someone to understand her.'

'She needs someone to put her in her place!'

For a few moments, his face was stern. Then he relaxed and reached out to touch Sonia's arm.

'But do not worry. This is your first day, and, since Elise is sulking, you must allow me to show you around the vine presses and explain how our wine is produced and stored.'

'Oh, that's kind of you but Edouard has already offered to show me around after we've had coffee. Has he gone already? I'd better catch up with him.'

She quickly gulped down her coffee and placed her cup on the table.

'Is it all right if I go out again, Veronique, or would you like me to help you prepare lunch?'

'No, no, no, Sonia. You are not here

to help me. Go with Paul. I can manage on my own. Besides, I will probably get Elise to help me.'

'Please tell Elise that I didn't mean to upset her and that I will speak to her later.'

'I will come with you, Sonia. Do you know much about the art of making wine and distilling the water of life?' Paul asked, standing up.

'No, but I'd like to.'

'Then you shall. Come!'

Edouard was nowhere to be seen, so it was Paul who showed Sonia the new, modern press, the fermenting tanks, and the gas-fired copper pots that had replaced the former coal-fired ones.

'These are made of pure copper,' he said with pride. 'They are very expensive but they withstand the acid in the wine and last much longer than the cheaper, impure ones.'

'Why are they empty? Is wine-making not a continual process like English ale brewing?'

'No. It is seasonally intensive. Throughout the winter, the vines have been pruned and relaid along wire frames in the vineyards. Soon, they will flower. This is the moment when the grapes are born and, from then on, the vines will require constant attention. They will be nurtured as tenderly as a mother nurtures her child.'

He turned to smile at her.

'Edouard will have to desert his many girl friends and will be held captive by a more demanding mistress! He must know the night-time temperature and light the torches, if necessary, to keep away the cold. He must remove excess foliage to give the developing grapes more light and he must choose the exact moment when the grapes are ready, slightly under-ripe for distilling, leaving only the ones for our own wine-making to mature further.'

'So, when does the harvest take place?'

'Three months after the flowering, usually at the beginning of October and through November. The fermentation takes one or two weeks, then the process is halted until we start the distilling. Once we start, the stills are kept busy day and night either until all of the wine has been distilled twice or until the last day of May, the last lawful date when wine produced in the autumn may be distilled.'

'It all sounds very complicated. Does it take a long time to learn how to do it all?'

'Not at all! It's in the blood. I come from a long line of vine growers. I was brought up with it as my heritage.'

Sonia laughed.

'Now you are trying to make it look easy, but I'm sure it's not!'

She was finding the tour fascinating.

'Of course, the difficult part is in the blending of the various distillations, all of which are taken only from officially approved vines,' Paul continued. 'There are many regulations to fulfil. Of course, not all wine-makers have their own distillery. You will know the ones that do their own distilling by the black fungus on the roofs. The fungus thrives on the vapours that are given off by the distilled wines. This is known as the Angels' Share. A romantic notion, is it not?' he added with a smile. 'Here, we not only distil our own wine but that from a number of nearby vineyards as well. It is a heavy responsibility.'

Paul's pride in his heritage was evident. No wonder he seemed so arrogant at times, she reflected. He bore a heavy responsibility without having had the benefit of having his parents to rear and guide him. In the normal run of things, Paul's father would have still been in charge, though she was sure Jerome and Veronique must have ably filled his parents' place.

She realised that Paul was smiling down at her.

'I think I would like to introduce you to our famous French wines.'

He tilted her chin up towards him.

'You would enjoy learning, yes?'

He leaned closer, the slight fragrance

of his aftershave arousing her senses. For a fleeting moment, she thought he was going to kiss her and her heart suddenly started to beat erratically, but he didn't. His smile widened and she felt her cheeks going hot.

'Yes, I would,' she stammered.

She didn't know whether or not it was the heady aroma in the building or her closeness to this commanding man but she was feeling definitely unsteady.

'Then we will arrange it.'

Back at the farm, she busied herself helping Veronique set the table for lunch and, afterwards, following a futile effort at striking up a conversation with Elise, she took herself outside and walked down to the field where the horses were grazing. It was a peaceful scene. Some of the horses came over to her and she wished she had taken some apples with her. As it was, she contented herself with stroking their noses and talking to them. How much simpler life would be if humans were as trusting and uncomplicated.

The afternoon passed slowly. Elise was subdued and asked for time alone to rest. Sonia helped Veronique. The older woman seemed glad of some company and encouraged Sonia to talk about her family, exclaiming volubly, throwing her hands in the air at some of her brothers' antics. Eventually, Veronique shooed her upstairs to have a rest before it was time to change for dinner. When she came downstairs dressed once again in her one and only dress, she found Paul waiting for her.

'You are very beautiful,' he murmured, reaching into a pocket and bringing out a gold chain with a ruby pendant dangling on it. 'This was my mother's,' he told her, holding the chain in front of her. 'Will you wear it tonight?'

Her eyes widened. The pendant was beautiful, but was it right for her to wear it? She had only known him for one day. Paul sensed her misgivings.

'It is of no significance, other than I always think that a beautiful woman should wear beautiful jewellery. I will be honoured by your acceptance.'

Sonia was in a dilemma. What should she do?

'Turn around and I will fasten it on you.'

She did as Paul suggested. She was facing a mirror on the wall and she watched her reflection as Paul reached around her, placing the pendant against her skin. He was right. It did look beautiful and it enhanced her own beauty. The touch of his fingers against her neck was electrifying. Instinctively, she raised her eyes and met the reflection of Paul's eyes in the mirror. She could read admiration there, and something else.

'It's lovely,' she said nervously, turning to face him. 'Are you sure?'

Before he could reply, the outer door opened and Edouard came striding through. He stopped abruptly as he saw them. Sonia saw his glance flicker towards the pendant and back to her face. Without consciously thinking about it, her hand flew to touch the pendant and she suddenly wished she hadn't agreed to wear it.

5

The tense atmosphere at dinner made Sonia feel very uncomfortable. Was this to be the daily pattern, or was it because she was wearing Paul's mother's necklet?

As she carefully spread some home-made pâté on to thin toast she glanced around the table. Veronique was decidedly uneasy; Edouard looked annoyed; Elise still had a defiant air about her; and, for some reason, Paul kept sending Edouard a look she could only describe as triumphant. Only Jerome seemed oblivious to it all. Surely her presence here with them wasn't the cause of their lack of harmony!

Edouard asked polite questions about her family, which she seized upon gratefully and amused them with more tales of her younger brothers. Even Elise was seen to smile briefly, though

Sonia noticed how quickly she managed to slip back into her self-imposed indifference. Not wanting to prolong the agony, as soon as Veronique made a move to clear away the final dishes, Sonia leaped to her feet and insisted on helping.

'I help at home,' she explained, 'so please allow me to help here.'

She found it easier to speak naturally in the kitchen and Veronique seemed to find it easier to chide the actions of her son and nephew out of their hearing.

'They have always been very competitive,' she excused them. 'I suppose it is because they were born on the same day. If Edouard ever did something first, Paul wouldn't rest until he had achieved it also.'

'And is Edouard as competitive towards Paul?'

Veronique considered for a moment.

'I think so, but he doesn't make such a show of it. He doesn't seem to have to prove himself quite so much.'

'I suppose that is because Paul is the

head of the family and feels he has to deserve his position as much by effort as by right,' Sonia mused aloud.

Veronique turned away to dry her hands.

'I expect you are right,' she said over her shoulder.

Sonia began to gather together the crockery for the morning's breakfast.

'Just place them on the table and cover them with this cloth, and then we are finished. You must now excuse me. I do not like to keep late hours. I must help Elise get ready for bed and then I, too, will retire.'

Sonia would have liked to have the opportunity to try to talk to Elise but, since that was now out of the question, she, too, made her excuses and went upstairs.

When she came downstairs the following day, only Jerome was seated at the breakfast table. He wasn't a great talker but he chatted with Sonia as they ate together, telling her of some of the jobs that he did in the vineyard.

'But you must ask Edouard if you wish to learn more. He is the one who keeps everything running so well. We have doubled our production since he took over the management side. Teaching him all I know was a father's pleasure and he has far surpassed even my highest expectations. But now, you must excuse me. Edouard will be wondering what is keeping me. I hope you have a pleasant day.'

Sonia was surprised by his words. Surely Paul was the driving force. Then she smiled. A father's pride in his son was not such a strange thing, was it? As he reached the door, Jerome turned back.

'Veronique will be with you soon. She had another bad night but she is on her way.'

Her breakfast completed, Sonia began to wonder what to do next. She washed the dishes that were waiting by the sink and tidied the table for its late occupants. She could hear movements upstairs but no-one else had yet joined her in the kitchen. She presumed Paul was already outside with Jerome and Edouard, so it must be Veronique still upstairs, which meant that Elise must still be waiting for her mother to assist her to get dressed. She wondered if Elise would allow her to help her. She hadn't made any overtures in that direction but if Veronique was finding things a bit difficult at the moment it could relieve some of the pressure on her, and, possibly, make a bridge across to Elise at the same time.

Nothing ventured, nothing gained, had been one of her grandmother's favourite phrases so Sonia decided to act upon her thought. She hesitated outside the door but couldn't hear any sounds. She knocked gently.

'Elise?' she called. 'May I come in?'

To her surprise it was Veronique who opened the door.

'What is it, Sonia? Is something wrong?'

'No, I'm sorry. I thought you were still upstairs, Veronique. I came to see if

I could be of any help to Elise.'

She instinctively looked beyond Veronique into the room as she spoke, realising too late that Elise was seated on a commode.

'Get away! Get out of here!' Elise screamed. 'How dare you come prying? I do not want you! Send her away, Maman!'

Sonia felt the blood drain from her face as she backed away.

'I'm sorry,' she whispered.

Veronique looked uncomfortable.

'It is very difficult, Sonia. Elise is very . . . '

'Do not talk about me as if I am not here!' Elise screamed again. 'Tell her to go! I don't want her here!'

Sonia turned quickly and almost ran back to the kitchen, very upset. She hadn't intended to cause offence or embarrassment to Elise. She should have given it more thought before she had acted, she now realised. Blinded by unshed tears, she ran straight into a strong, masculine body.

'Hey! What's the matter?'

Edouard's voice was compassionate. Sonia knew that sympathy would open the floodgates of her tears so she tried to push past him. He held on to her, pulling her back gently towards him. He insisted on lifting her chin so that he could see her face, even though she tried to bury her face in his shirt. She knew the tears of humiliation were already brimming over. This was ridiculous! Why was she upset? Elise had every right to refuse her untimely offer of help.

'Here! Use this.'

A white handkerchief was being wafted in front of her.

'Thank you.'

'Has my sister hurt you?'

'It's my own fault. I didn't stop to think. I embarrassed Elise.'

She dabbed at her eyes as she spoke, feeling better already.

'It was stupid of me to take it badly! I'm all right now. Thanks for listening.'

'Have you had your breakfast?'

'Yes.'

'Good. Why don't you come out with me for an hour or so? I don't think Elise will object to me stealing you from her, do you?'

He managed to elicit a smile from her.

'I'm just about to inspect some of the vines. I'm sure you will find it interesting, and it will give me the opportunity to make it up to you for deserting you yesterday. Did Paul explain that he asked me to take his place at a meeting with some other vintners of the area?'

Sonia blinked in amazement, but felt too confused to make a direct reply. What exactly had Paul said? She couldn't really remember but felt sure he had led her to believe that he didn't know where Edouard had gone. She was puzzled, but merely shook her head.

'Paul took me round the wine press area and to the distilling cellar. It was very interesting. I hope I am still here when the grapes are ready to be pressed.'

Her voice sounded too bright but, to her relief, Edouard didn't pursue the question. He simply smiled and ushered her out into the courtyard ahead of him. The sun was already rising high in the brilliant blue sky. The air smelled fresh and clean. One of the peacocks shrieked loudly, receiving an answering call from across the courtyard. It was going to be a beautiful day. They went past the stables towards a field where some horses were grazing. Edouard stopped suddenly and looked at her enquiringly.

'You did say you can ride, didn't you?'

'A little. Why?'

'Just a thought. Shall we ride to the vineyards? It would be very pleasant.'

He smiled down at her, causing her heart to leap. What was it about these two cousins? Both of them seemed to set her heart beating fast. Was it purely a physical reaction? There was no doubt that they were extremely good-looking and, on the outside, as identical as made no difference. But, inside? They both excited her senses, but they were like the opposite sides of a coin. Paul thrilled and challenged her, a dangerous liaison, whereas Edouard's presence gave a sense of peace and caring. The way he was now smiling at her was as if the thought of riding with her was the most important thing in the world to him. Her heart leaped. It would be nice. She nodded.

'Why not?'

They retraced their steps to the tackle room. A stable lad hurried out of the inner room but Edouard waved him away.

'We'll saddle up ourselves, Alex.'

He turned to Sonia.

'Find a hat that fits. I'll get your saddle. I think Papillon will be a good mount for you. She is very gentle and doesn't mind different riders.'

Sonia found a hat that fitted well and took the saddle that Edouard handed to her. In no time at all, he was back at her side with his own heavier saddle in his arms.

'Is that all right for you?' he asked, nodding towards the saddle. 'Not too heavy?'

'No. I can manage. I'm not a weakling!'

He grinned.

'I didn't presume you were. I would not have engaged a weakling to look after my headstrong sister.'

They walked in companionable silence the rest of the way back to the field. Edouard rested his saddle on top of the fence before vaulting over it. He strode out into the field towards the group of horses quietly cropping the grass. Sonia leaned her arms along the top of the fence and rested her chin on them. A sense of peace flowed into her. Whatever the cause of the discord in this family, there was something about the place that bound them together, and she found herself being drawn into it. She couldn't explain the feeling, neither could she expand on it. She just knew she was needed here.

Edouard was on his way back, leading two horses. The smaller one was mid-brown with a white butterfly-shaped dash on her nose. She snickered gently and blew down her nose as Sonia reached out to stroke her.

'I'll saddle her for you,' Edouard offered. 'Next time, I will let you do it.'

He tossed the saddle on to Papillon's back and fastened the straps.

'Talk to her, whilst I saddle Majeur.'

Sonia held the bridle under Papillon's chin, stroking her long nose and talking endearments. Papillon nuzzled into her, snickering and snuffling.

'I've nothing for you.' Sonia laughed. 'I'll bring you an apple next time.'

'Here! Catch!'

Edouard tossed an apple to her.

'You will learn never to come without one. We have hundreds in the store-room. Are you ready to mount?'

'Yes.'

She was thankful that she had a little experience and managed quite a graceful mount. As Edouard had predicted, Papillon was easy to ride and she felt comfortable from the start. Edouard himself mounted in a graceful, fluid movement that left her gasping.

'Shall we canter round the field to give the horses some exercise first?' he suggested. 'Majeur will be aggrieved if he doesn't have the opportunity to show off a little!'

Sonia agreed and they took pleasure in twenty minutes or so of relaxed riding.

'Did you enjoy that?' Edouard asked. 'Your cheeks are rosy now.'

Sonia blushed, making them more so.

'Yes, it was good. I am not as proficient as you,' she added apologetically.

'You have quite a good seat and, with practice, you will improve. Feel free to ride whenever you wish. One of the stable lads will go with you until you get to know the best places to go and I will be pleased to join you whenever I can. You never know, we may be able to persuade Elise to ride again eventually. She is afraid, I think.'

Sonia agreed. They were heading out towards the vineyards, walking the horses side by side. Edouard pointed out various landmarks that bordered their land, passing comments as he did so. He talked of their work force and their families, revealing his deep interest and care for them in his personal knowledge of them. When they reached the part where the current work was going on, he greeted each one as they passed or stopped for a word or two with those nearby, explaining to Sonia the whys and wherefores of what they were doing.

At one place, they dismounted and he showed her the shoulder-high frameworks of wire that supported the vines, showing her how the new growth had been curved round and fastened into place in early spring, forming the most effective shape for healthy fruit to grow.

'Later, many of the leaves will be trimmed back, to give more sunlight to the swelling grapes.'

'Why do you need to inspect the vines so often?' Sonia asked.

'We need to know exactly when the vines flower, so that we know exactly when to harvest. Wine used in the distillation of cognac has to have been meticulously monitored throughout, right from the choosing of the vines, through its planting, nurturing and harvesting even to the type of vessel the liquid is stored in and the time allowed for the distillations. Only the varieties of vines agreed upon are planted. No irrigation is allowed. The resulting liquid is distilled twice and then the various distillations are carefully blended to retain the exact taste of finished cognac.'

'Why so much care? Isn't it expected that each year will have its own distinctive flavour? You know, like people taste the wine they order in a restaurant and pronounce it acceptable or not?'

'With wines, yes, but cognac must always taste the same, year after year, decade after decade, even century after century. That is why the blending is so important. The man in charge of the blending — we call him the cellar-man, though that doesn't show the depth of his knowledge and experience — must educate his palate so that he is able to decide, almost by instinct, how much of each individual distillation must go into each blending. My father admits that he can only train me to a certain extent. To go further, I will have to train with one of the houses of cognac, if they decide that I am worth taking on.'

Sonia frowned.

'Does Paul do this also? He gave me the impression that the instinct you speak of is passed more by inherited genes than by actual training.'

Edouard was silent for a moment. Sonia had to look at his face to determine whether or not he had heard. Edouard tightened his lips.

'Paul has had the same opportunities as I have to train his palate, more so, if anything. My father has tried to pass on to him whatever knowledge Paul's father, my Uncle Yves, would have passed on to him. But, Paul prefers to trust in his own preference and, consequently, lacks consistency. Fortunately, that has no bearing on what we prepare and sell on to the cognac houses. The blending comes later, within the cognac houses themselves.'

'Do you mind being the younger one?' she asked impulsively, aware that Edouard's dedication to the whole affair went far deeper than Paul's.

Edouard smiled.

'I am the elder one, actually. But my father was the younger twin, so Paul inherited the position as soon as he was born. His father, Uncle Yves, had died a few months earlier. Our mothers went into labour on the same day. I was born first, then about an hour later, Paul was born, but Aunt Yvette died in child-birth. As to whether or not I mind Paul's position, the answer is no. We knew about it from the start. My parents raised us together and lavished as much love on Paul as on me.'

A sadness came into his eyes and he looked away into the distance for a moment. He grimaced wryly.

'At times, it seemed to me that it were more towards Paul, you know, as if to assure him that they really meant it, especially my mother. I know he hurts her at times by his seeming disregard. He seems to feel he was abandoned by his real parents, instead of them having died. At times, I don't understand him, but who knows how I would feel if things were reversed. Such complexities are what make us as we are.'

They sat in silence for a moment, both lost in their own thoughts. Sonia felt she had more insight into Paul's character, wondering how different he might have been if his parents had lived. Edouard smiled suddenly, lightening the atmosphere.

'I apologise, Sonia. I should not burden you with our family problems. You are so easy to talk to. Please forgive me.'

When they returned to the house for lunch, Sonia was pleased to find that her luggage had been delivered. At last, she had her own clothes to wear and her own luxuries of life, such as her personal toiletry items and some paperback novels and magazines she had packed. Determined to spend time with Elise in the afternoon, she suggested that they read one of the magazines together and selected one that had an article on hair care. After a hesitant start, the session went better than Sonia had dared hope and, at the end of it, when she offered to wash Elise's hair, the girl agreed.

She felt a bit tense as she applied the shampoo, in case it stung Elise's eyes, but by the time she was blow-drying she began to relax. Elise had chosen a spikey style and they were giggling like schoolgirls by the time Sonia had combed in some styling gel and was teasing each lock of hair into separate spikes. Elise watched every move in the mirror, her eyes gleaming with suppressed mischief.

'I hope you are sure about this style, Elise,' Sonia warned. 'Your mother is going to be shocked, I'm sure.'

'And Paul? Will he be shocked, do you think?'

Sonia was aware that Elise was testing her reaction and tried to reply in an off-hand manner.

'I'm sure he'll notice,' she said coolly.

'And Edouard?'

'He'll laugh!'

'Ah! You are beginning to sort them out. Have you come to any decision as to whom you prefer?'

Her glance was full of challenge. Sonia blushed.

'I needn't prefer either, need I?'

'No, but I'll be surprised if you don't! Now, help me get dressed before you dress yourself, then Maman will not see my hair until dinner, then I can shock everyone together.'

She stopped suddenly and a red blush spread over her cheeks.

'By the way, I'm sorry about this morning. I felt so embarrassed. It can be quite . . . I don't know the English word for it.'

'Belittling?' Sonia suggested.

'Belittling, then, to have every personal action seen by someone else.'

Sonia touched her arm impulsively.

'I was the one at fault. I should have given it more thought.'

They smiled at each other. Sonia sensed they had taken a valuable step towards each other.

6

Veronique was surprised at the request from Sonia to dress Elise for dinner but willingly agreed to it.

'Elise is coming round to accepting you, and it will help me out a little as well,' she admitted.

She was leaning wearily against the drainer at the sink, trying to peel the vegetables. Sonia coaxed her to a chair and made a pot of tea. Brushing aside Veronique's protests, she peeled the potatoes and carrots, put them on the stove and checked that the meat was already cooking.

'I'll be all right now, Sonia,' Veronique told her. 'Life's been a bit hectic since Elise's accident. I think it's all catching up with me now that it's all easing off. You've been a good help to me and with Elise. I'm very grateful.'

By the time Elise was dressed, Sonia had only twenty minutes left to see to herself. She quickly showered, then chose a pale blue sundress, twisted her hair and fastened it at the back of her head and applied a little make-up. Some loose tendrils of hair escaped their confines and sprang back to frame her face. She added a pair of pearl, tear-drop earrings, feeling much easier with them than the gold pendant of the previous day.

As she went downstairs, she could hear another female voice mingling with those of Jerome, Paul and Edouard. It wasn't Elise. The young woman with them was slightly built. Her long, straight fair hair fell freely, framing her classically beautiful face. She was laughing in response to some remark, her hand lying casually on Paul's arm. Sonia smiled as she stepped towards them. Jerome noticed her first and held out his hand to draw her forwards.

'Ah, Sonia, may I present Corrine

Lebrun? She is . . . er . . . a family friend.'

Sonia noticed a slight hesitation and wondered what it signified. Corrine turned and smiled coolly. Sonia felt she detected a warning in the smile, making her wonder if one of the Blaise cousins regarded her especially as his. Veronique's entrance, wheeling in the dinner-trolley, distracted her thoughts. The older woman looked enquiringly at Sonia.

'Is Elise ready?'

'I expect so. I left her putting on her make-up. Shall I check?'

Jerome restrained her.

'Leave her. She knows what time we have dinner. You are not here to run around after her. Sit down, everyone.'

'Why exactly are you here?' Corrine asked Sonia. 'A sort of au pair?'

'Not at all,' Edouard said. 'Sonia is here as an English tutor for Elise.'

'Oh, dear. Are we all to speak English at dinner? I'm afraid I am not as fluent as these two.'

Corrine looked fondly between Paul and Edouard.

'I will need extra tuition myself. Which one of you will give it to me, I wonder.'

Her voice was light but Sonia couldn't quite decide whether she was teasing or flirting. Both men smiled but it was Paul who offered her his arm and led her to the table. Edouard's glance followed them and Sonia was surprised to see a wry expression on his face. Then he turned to her and made an elaborate bow before offering her his arm. She laughed, glad to have the mood lightened. They had just seated themselves when Elise made her entrance.

There was a shocked silence, and Sonia nearly choked. Elise had added sparkly, blue glitter to her spiked hair. Her eyes were surrounded by blue and purple eye-shadow and blue gloss covered her lips.

'Ooh, la, la!' Veronique exclaimed, her hands raised in mock horror.

'Elise, I will not have you looking like that at our dinner table!' Jerome reprimanded her.

Paul's face set angrily as he exclaimed, 'Go back and wash it off! You look like a clown!'

'Oh, leave her,' Corrine pleaded. 'She looks sweet!'

Elise grinned unconcernedly.

'You'd better get used to it. This is the real me! What about you, Edouard? What do you think?'

Edouard's grin matched Elise's own.

'You look incredible! Let her be, Papa. She is doing no harm.'

The general atmosphere was lighter than on the two previous evenings and, once the meal was over, everyone stayed together longer. It was Veronique who was the first to break up the party.

'My bed calls,' she apologised. 'Come on, Elise, I'm sorry, but I'll have to get you ready for bed now.'

'Oh, Maman, not yet!' she exclaimed and turned eagerly to Sonia. 'Will you help me?'

'Of course.'

'All right, but don't stay up too late,' Veronique warned.

Jerome retired with his wife, leaving the younger ones to themselves. Sonia enjoyed the lighthearted conversation, though, at times, she wondered if there were undercurrents that she wasn't privy to. She tried to weigh up which of the two cousins Corrine was involved with.

Surely it was Paul whom Corrine seemed more attached to, yet she flirted coyly with Edouard also and seemed disappointed by his lack of response. Was she trying to make him jealous for some reason? If anything, Edouard seemed to be more embarrassed than jealous. Was that on Paul's behalf, since Corrine was his girlfriend? Or had Corrine not yet made up her mind which of the two cousins she liked the most?

Sonia could identify with that! Paul was more challenging, more exciting, but she also found herself feeling uneasy about him. She wasn't sure she completely trusted him. He seemed to enjoy playing games with people's emotions, and she didn't intend to satisfy him by falling for his charms.

On the other hand, Edouard was easy to like. She marvelled that he already meant so much to her. She found herself waiting to hear his voice and see his eyes crinkle into a smile when he looked at her.

'What did you think of Corrine?' Elise asked her later, as Sonia was helping her to undress. 'She is very pretty, isn't she?'

'Yes, she is. Tell me, whose friend is she? I couldn't quite decide.'

Elise laughed harshly.

'A month ago, she was Edouard's girlfriend. We all thought they were planning to become engaged, then Corrine told him that she had fallen in love with Paul.'

'Oh, no! Was Edouard very upset?'

Elise shrugged.

'I think so, but he hides his feelings

better than Paul.'

'And Paul? Does he feel the same about Corrine?'

'I don't know, but if he thinks Edouard still loves her, he will go along with it, for as long as it suits him.'

So, Edouard was nursing a broken heart. The pang of sadness she felt took her by surprise. In all honesty, she acknowledged to herself that it was tinged with a note of jealousy that his heart was yearning for someone else. She realised that she was beginning to feel more for Edouard than she had thought. But he obviously needed time to sort out his feelings for Corrine before he would be free to want a relationship with anyone else.

Life settled down over the next few days and things seemed to be running smoothly. Feeling that she had nothing to do whilst Elise was with her physiotherapist in the afternoons, Sonia offered to do some clerical work in the office. Edouard leaped at the offer.

'It does rather mount up,' he admitted. 'Maman used to do a few hours but, since Elise's accident, she hasn't had time, or the energy,' he added. 'I'm a bit worried about her, Sonia. She is always tired. Do you think there could be something wrong with her? Apart from just being tired, that is.'

Sonia considered carefully but had to admit that she didn't really know.

'She's had a lot to do, running the house and looking after Elise's personal needs. I wish Elise would let me help, but, since she won't, at least I can help in this other way. What needs doing most?'

'Come to the office. I will show you.'

The room they used as an office was farther along the main ground-floor passageway past Elise's room. It over-looked the courtyard at the back of the house. One glance showed that the work there had been neglected of late. Edouard grimaced.

'It is a bit messy, isn't it? Do you

think you can sort it out?'

'Yes, I'm sure I can. Any particular order to it?'

'File wine orders then payments, queries, government letters, then put any you're not sure about into a miscellaneous box. Have you got much experience with one of these?' he asked, pointing to the computer.

'Some, as long as the programme is already set up. What about letter replies? Do you want me to do some rough drafts?'

'That's a good idea. Do what you can and I'll come back later and show you the software programme we use and check what you've done, not that I anticipate having to correct much, just as a safety net, you understand.' He smiled warmly. 'You have already made a big difference to life here.'

'That's what I'm here for. Shall I start right away?'

'If you wish. The sooner it's sorted the better! I really am grateful. Don't forget to give yourself a break and if

Maman or Elise need you for anything, leave this.'

Edouard left her to it and Sonia began to sort through the piles of correspondence and other papers on the desk. It wasn't too complicated and, after an hour or so, most of the correspondence had been sorted. Hearing a sound in the doorway, she turned round, smiling a welcome.

'I've nearly done the sorting. Shall I start on the replies now?'

'What are you doing in here?'

It was Paul, she realised.

'I offered to help in here whilst Elise is with the physiotherapist. Edouard said it would be a big help.'

'I bet he did! Covering his own negligence in letting it slip into this mess!'

'Things haven't been easy since Elise's accident. Veronique has her time taken up with the extra work,' Sonia defended the need for her help. 'Besides, I really don't mind. In fact, I'm grateful for something extra to do. I want to pull my weight whilst I'm here.'

Paul moved a step nearer, his face softening.

'Don't let my cousin take advantage of you. I'm sure I can find better ways for you to spend your afternoons. I hear you went riding with Edouard the other day. Would you like to come out riding with me? There are some lovely places I could show you.'

He leaned casually against the desk, his mouth curled into a smile.

'That's very kind of you. I would enjoy that, but, not today,' she replied diplomatically. 'I'd like to get everything in order here first. I promised.'

'Do you always keep your promises?' Paul asked provocatively.

He leaned forward and lifted her chin with his forefinger, searching the depths of her eyes for her response. She knew he was teasing her and it made her feel uncomfortable. What was it that made her react so differently to this man than to his identical cousin? If this was Edouard, she would be hoping he might kiss her. As it was . . .

Paul let go and stood up abruptly. Had he seen the lack of response in her eyes?

'Don't try to play me off against Edouard,' he warned, 'not if you intend to impress me.'

'I've no intention of playing either of you against the other. I'm here to work, to help Elise.'

She kept her voice steady, thankful that she was sitting down. Her legs might have given way under her, otherwise.

'Now, if you'll allow me to get on, please.'

'What's this?' Paul asked sharply, picking up a paper from the top of the miscellaneous box.

She half-rose to glance at the paper he was waving in front of her.

'I'm not sure. That's why I put it in there. It seems like a memo to cover someone's work. Allain Mouille, isn't it? I expect Edouard can explain it.'

'He'd better! I don't pay him to cover

for other people! No wonder his own job is in such a mess! Tell him I want an explanation!'

With that, he pushed the paper into his pocket and strode off, letting the door bang to behind him. Sonia stared at the door, feeling very perturbed. Why was he so angry? Surely if Edouard wished to cover for someone, he had a good reason.

She continued with the work, making a start on some of the letters but, when Edouard didn't come to check them, she saved them on to the computer hard-drive, backed them up on a disk and closed the office. It was time for her to see if Elise or Veronique needed any help.

Elise's room was empty, so she moved on towards the kitchen. Hearing raised voices, she realised that Edouard was home and that Paul was already demanding an explanation about the memo. Her heart sank. Did Paul always conduct his affairs this way? She was relieved that the shouting was all in

Paul's voice, which meant that Edouard had kept cool. Even so, it wasn't the best way to go about things.

From the other subdued voices, she gathered that they weren't alone, then she heard Jerome say, 'Allain has given us good work over ten years. This isn't the way to repay him.'

'I won't do it!' Edouard stated firmly.

'This isn't right, Paul. Please reconsider!' Veronique's tearful voice pleaded.

Sonia hesitated. It didn't seem right to intrude into a family dispute but before she had decided what to do, the door was wrenched open. Paul's hand was on the handle but he still had his back towards her. Beyond, she could see the distressed faces of the rest of the family.

'Just see to it, will you, or you might find yourselves in the same predicament!' Paul hurled at them as he left.

7

Paul strode out, nearly knocking Sonia aside. She stared after him — then back into the kitchen. The rest of the family was there. Jerome's face was red with anger. Veronique was white and very shaky. Edouard was helping her to a chair. Elise looked anxious.

'What did he mean, Papa? He can't sack us, can he? We live here. It is partly our farm, too, isn't it?'

Jerome sighed heavily.

'Yes, but he can make life very awkward for us. My brother would never have allowed this. We have always looked after our workers, not kicked them whilst they are down.'

Veronique began to cry.

'It is my fault,' She sobbed. 'I shouldn't have done it.'

Edouard folded her in his arms.

'Nonsense, Maman. You were not to

know. See, I will sweep it all up.'

It was only then that Sonia saw a smashed casserole dish on the floor, its contents spilled and scattered. She stepped forward.

'I'll do that,' she offered. 'Did it fall?'

'You might say so,' Edouard replied coldly. 'Maman had made it for Allain Mouille's family, to help them out whilst Madame Mouille is ill in hospital. For some reason, Paul took great exception to it and demands that we sack Allain. He also knows I have been covering his work for him, so it wasn't your fault, Maman.'

'Ah!'

Sonia understood and told them how Paul had discovered the incident.

'I'm sorry if I've somehow caused this row.'

Edouard shook his head.

'It's not your fault. He would have found out sometime.'

'What will you do about it?'

Sonia looked from Edouard to Jerome. Edouard thumped his clenched fist on the table.

'We'll do nothing! There is no way I am going to sack Allain Mouille! He is a good worker and when his wife is better and home again, he will give us all the hours we ask of him.'

He looked carefully at both his parents.

'Are you in complete agreement with me? Paul will puff and steam about it for a while and make us all feel that we are living on tenterhooks. Can you put up with that? Can you, Maman? It won't be too much for you, the way you feel so tired at the moment?'

Veronique wiped her eyes.

'Whatever you say, Edouard. You are a good, good son to me.'

Paul was heard to leave, over-revving his car engine, making a noisy exit. His departure lightened the atmosphere and they decided to eat their evening meal in the kitchen for once. It was a pleasant evening. Everyone relaxed and it wasn't long before laughter was ringing out. Sonia was aware that

Edouard glanced at her often and she met his eyes with a smile, knowing Elise would tease her about it later.

Eventually, Veronique was persuaded to go to bed and after Jerome had checked up that everything was locked up outside, he followed her. Sonia organised clearing away the dishes, whilst Edouard began to wash them and Elise dried them.

'We are no strangers to this,' Edouard assured her, looking very much at home with his arms covered in suds. 'We used to fight for the chore of washing because the one who washed finished first!' he added in response to Sonia's puzzled look.

'Of course, Paul used to pull rank!' Elise added. 'Especially if he had a date!'

'Let's leave him out of it for tonight,' Edouard suggested, smiling apologetically towards Sonia. 'He'll be fine in the morning. Now, I think you should be getting Elise off to bed. My little sister is looking tired.'

'Yes, big brother!'

Elise flicked her tea-towel at him.

'What! No argument?'

'Not tonight. You are right, and I go to see Dr Mathoux tomorrow. I wonder what he will say.'

★   ★   ★

Elise and Edouard were seated at the kitchen table already eating their breakfast when Sonia arrived downstairs the following day. Veronique was busy kneading a batch of dough and Jerome was putting on his boots.

'Bonjour,' she greeted them, smiling at Veronique. 'Are you feeling better today, Veronique?'

'Ah, so, so! We needed an early start. Elise's appointment is at ten.'

'Don't overdo it,' Jerome warned as he went out. 'See you tonight, Edouard, Elise.'

'We wondered if you would like to come to Cognac with us, Sonia,' Edouard proposed. 'It's a lovely town and well worth a visit. I am taking Elise to see her spinal specialist but that takes only a short time. Then, whilst I meet with some of the vine growers there, you and Elise will be able to look around together.'

'Oh! That would be lovely!' Sonia responded.

'I'll give you both ten minutes,' Edouard added as they finished their breakfast. 'We need to leave at nine thirty sharp.'

Sonia changed into one of her sundresses and comfortable sandals then went to collect Elise who was ready to go.

'I think you had better push me!' Elise suggested. 'Edouard will be waiting for us.'

At the foot of the stairs they almost mowed down Paul.

'Do not stop us,' Elise cried. 'We must hurry or Edouard will be cross.'

Sonia swivelled the wheel-chair through the kitchen doorway, casting only an apologetic look at Paul as she passed him. He seemed rather bemused. She wondered whether or not she should have explained where they were going but knew it would delay their progress. Besides, she was simply doing her job in accompanying Elise to Cognac. She was sure she didn't have to explain her every move. Nevertheless, she felt a little uncomfortable and when she glanced over her shoulder, the expression on Paul's face was one of annoyance. Maybe he had thought her behaviour to be too frivolous. Well, that was his problem, not hers!

Edouard lifted Elise carefully out of her wheel-chair and placed her on the back seat of the car, wrapping a blanket around her legs. Sonia seated herself in the front passenger seat. She was looking forward to the day out.

At the hospital she was surprised when Edouard asked her to accompany them into the consultation room. She glanced quickly at Elise to see her reaction. She was twisting her hands together, her head down. Then she looked up. Sonia could see fear in her eyes.

'Yes, please, come,' she whispered softly. 'If you are going to help me, you need to know what the doctor has to say.'

After carefully examining Elise, the doctor seated himself in front of her.

'There is nothing physically wrong now,' he told her gently. 'The bones in your legs are healed and, as far as I can see, your spinal injuries have mended also. I would like you to start trying to stand up for short periods. No-one will put any pressure on you to go beyond what you feel capable of doing,' the doctor assured her, 'but your muscles will benefit from being used. Your masseuse will help you. Will you try?'

Silently, Elise nodded.

'Good! I shall look forward to your next visit. Make an appointment with my secretary on your way out.'

Once outside, Edouard made arrangements to meet them mid-afternoon and then had to hurry away to his meeting with the other wine growers, leaving Sonia and Elise to arrange their own plan for the day.

'I will show you around the town,' Elise offered, 'but you will have to push me, I'm afraid. In the old part of town the streets are cobbled and some of them are very steep.'

Sonia was more than willing. She looked upon it as a means of building up the friendship growing between them. Elise kept up a running commentary as they set off through the old streets, pointing out the now familiar blackened roofs and giving historical details of the fortunes of Cognac. They eventually emerged through a mediaeval gateway with walls more than two metres thick, on to the banks of the river.

'Shall we rest here for a while?' Elise suggested. 'You have pushed my wheel-chair for over an hour and I know it is not easy.'

Sonia was ready for a rest and she gratefully parked the wheel-chair next to one of the many seats along the riverbank. Not having much money, and being reluctant to ask for any, Sonia had bought two baguettes well filled with country ham and salad for their lunch and they sat in companionable silence as they munched them.

It was Elise who spoke first.

'Were you surprised by what my doctor said?' she asked.

'Which bit?' Sonia asked.

'When he said that there is no reason why I cannot walk.'

She was sitting hunched in her wheel-chair, her face averted.

'Well, a bit, I suppose. But I have read of similar cases in the past. There is usually some underlying reason why it happens. What do you think?'

Elise was silent for a moment as she considered the question. When she replied, her voice was sharp.

'I do want to walk again. I hate it in this thing! People look at me with pity in their eyes and sometimes talk about me as though I am not there. I feel like screaming at them that I am neither deaf nor stupid! But I know they don't understand. How can they, if they have never been trapped in a wheelchair themselves?'

Sonia reflected her own attitude.

'I may have been guilty of that in the past,' she confessed. 'Most people have never known anyone in a wheel-chair, so they are unprepared for it. Why do you think you can't walk?' she asked directly.

'I don't know. My parents want me to be ready to go to university in October, but I feel afraid. There will be so many people. Maybe the doctor is wrong. Do you think I am a fraud?'

Sonia reached out and touched Elise's arm.

'No, I don't. If the doctor is right, we'll work at it. We're all behind you.'

Elise seemed grateful for Sonia's unqualified support.

'You won't discuss this with Paul, will you? He thinks I'm making it up, just pretending I can't walk. But I'm not, honestly!'

'I believe you, Elise, and I'm sure Paul will, when Edouard explains.'

'No! Please, Sonia! Tell Edouard not to tell Paul!'

Elise sounded as if she were becoming hysterical. Sonia felt alarmed.

'I'll do what I can, Elise, but it must be Edouard's decision in the end. I've only been here a week or so. You can't expect me to have a great deal of influence over either of them.'

Elise smiled shyly.

'They both like you.'

'Don't be silly!'

'I'm not. They are like two dogs scrapping over a bone!'

Sonia laughed.

'They are a bit, aren't they? Tell me, Elise. How can you always tell one from the other so quickly? I still hesitate at times.'

'Just look at their eyes, Sonia. That will tell you.'

Elise studied her for a moment, then

grinned impishly.

'I think we are now friends, don't you, Sonia?'

The smile faded and she looked out across the river, suddenly withdrawn into herself again. Sonia touched her arm.

'What is it?' she asked gently.

Her eyebrows puckered for a moment, then, with a flash of insight, Sonia felt she knew.

'Don't your friends ever come to see you, Elise? I haven't heard you mention any.'

Elise continued to stare across the river but Sonia could tell she had tensed her whole body.

'I'm sorry. I shouldn't have asked.'

Elise remained silent for a number of seconds, then slowly turned to face Sonia. Her face was drawn, her eyes cold.

'I have no friends,' she stated flatly.

'What? An attractive girl like you? I'm sure you have.'

Elise bit her lip.

'I didn't want pity, so I told them not to come to see me.'

'And?'

'None of them came. Real friends would have come.'

'Well, maybe. But perhaps they didn't know what to do for the best.'

'They only wanted to talk about what they were doing — discos, clubs, boyfriends and things. What use are those things to me any more? They cared nothing about me.'

'I'm sure they did, but didn't know how to talk to you, and you probably didn't make it easy for them!'

'What do you know about it? You weren't here!'

A sudden flash of fire had lit Elise's eyes. Just when Sonia wondered if she had gone too far, the fire died.

'I couldn't bear to see them then. I felt ugly. But, now . . . '

She paused and looked down at her hands, twisting them together.

'I suppose I'd like to see them again, but I won't beg them to come.'

Sonia looked thoughtful.

'Maybe you could invite them to a party or something. I'm sure we could soon fix up something, with some music, a buffet. What do you say?'

A hopeful light shone in Elise's eyes.

'Do you think they'd come, after how I treated them?'

'I'm sure they will, and with your new hairstyle and trendy make-up, you'll knock 'em for six!'

'Pardon? Knock 'em for six? What is that?'

'Oh, give them a big surprise! Wow!'

Elise laughed.

'Let's do it!'

They met up with Edouard at the arranged time. Elise took herself off to look at some shoes in a nearby shop window, her meaningful look telling Sonia to make use of the time to persuade Edouard to keep the doctor's verdict to themselves for a little while longer. Sonia found herself looking at Edouard's eyes. They sent every bit as much of a shiver down her spine as

125

Paul's did. So, where was the difference, as Elise had indicated?

'Dark brown!'

Edouard's eyes were twinkling brightly as she stared at him, puzzled.

'Pardon?' she queried.

'My eyes are dark brown.'

'Yes. Oh! I'm sorry. How rude of me!'

'Not at all. I find it extremely delightful.'

They smiled at each other in mutual amusement, then Sonia burst out laughing. She decided to come clean.

'Elise said that she can tell which is you and which is Paul by your eyes, but I don't know what she means. You are both so alike! And you both have brown eyes.'

'We are alike on the outside, yes, but inside we are very much different. See it through our eyes.'

'Yes, but it takes time to get to know what someone is like on the inside, doesn't it?'

Edouard inclined his head.

'There's no hurry. I hope you will be here for many months.'

His arm was resting lightly on the back of the street bench where Elise had left them. He absently fingered her hair.

'I think you are making good progress with Elise. I haven't seen her so relaxed for a long time, not since her accident, in fact. But, she was acting a bit strange a few minutes ago. What has she persuaded you to speak to me about? A larger allowance?'

The close proximity of his eyes was having a most devastating effect on her. Maybe they were identical to Paul's but she could already detect a warmth there that brought a blush to her cheeks. Furious with herself, she moved away a few inches and took a deep breath.

'No. Nothing like that. She doesn't want us to tell Paul what the doctor said, though I think he suspects as much anyway. I think she wants to work on it by herself without being under too much pressure to make more progress than she feels able to cope with. Have I explained that well enough to make sense?'

To her relief, Edouard nodded.

'Paul is rather overbearing at times, I'm afraid, as head of the family and all that. I think we could be rather vague on what was said and hope no-one presses for details. In the meantime, we must try to encourage Elise to persevere with the physiotherapy and massages and hope we get somewhere. Will that satisfy her, do you think?'

Elise accepted that that was the best deal she could expect.

As the crowning touch to a lovely day out, Edouard phoned his mother to tell her not to cook dinner for them and he took them to a small restaurant he knew. Sonia felt that her friendship with Elise was on a much firmer footing and all three of them enjoyed a very pleasant time together.

It wasn't late when they returned but the facial expressions of Jerome and Paul made them feel that they had somehow incurred their displeasure.

'You have decided to return, then?' was Paul's icy greeting.

Edouard glanced at the clock on the mantelpiece.

'It is not late. What is the matter, Papa?'

Sonia watched in alarm and Elise suddenly cried out.

'Maman! Where is she?'

'Your mother is all right,' Jerome soothed his daughter. 'She has gone to bed, that's all.'

'We have a labour problem on our hands!' Paul declared sharply. 'While you have been out enjoying yourselves, our entire workforce has decided to withdraw its labour!'

Edouard looked at him blankly.

'What do you mean? What's happened?'

'Just what I say! Everyone has laid down their tools and gone! I have a good mind to sack the lot of them! First thing tomorrow morning I want you to get in touch with each one of them and tell them that if they aren't back here by ten o'clock, they can consider themselves fired!'

Edouard's eyes glinted with anger but he managed to keep control.

'What provoked their walk-out?' he asked quietly.

Paul tightened his mouth. It was the first time Sonia had seen him looking less than sure of himself.

'I did what you should have done days ago,' he said harshly. 'I told Allain Mouille that he no longer had a job with us. The man had the audacity to plead for time, and then to threaten me! We're well-rid of him!'

'He is in temporary difficulties, that is all,' Edouard excused him. 'I told you, his wife will be home next week and he will be able to return to his normal hours. He has a young family to look after. What do you expect him to do? Leave them on their own?'

'I expect him to make alternative arrangements. His family difficulties aren't our problem. If you hadn't tried to cover for him, this would have been avoided.'

'I disagree. I did no more than I would expect anyone in charge of an established family concern to do. Our men show great loyalty. The least we can do is offer them the same in return.'

'Huh! They haven't shown much loyalty by walking out, have they?'

'They only did that in response to your harshness. Some of them have worked longer hours to hold Allain's job open for him. Nothing has been left undone!'

'Then it shows we can do without him! I tell you, my patience is running low. Get it sorted, or you may find yourself on the scrap heap, as well!'

Edouard kept his gaze level.

'I will visit the men but I won't threaten them. We need them as much as they need us. I'm not prepared to lose our workforce over an incident like this.'

'You will be putting your whole

family in jeopardy. Are you prepared to do that over a mere worker?'

'It is your high-handed action that has put us in this position. That mere worker you talk about is a man such as you or I! I will do what I can to smooth things over.'

'You'll do as I tell you!'

The two men faced each other, neither prepared to back down.

'Stop it!' Elise shouted. 'Why do you never agree about anything?'

She directed the first of her words towards Paul but she included Edouard in her glare. Her body sagged.

'I'm tired. I want to go to bed.'

'Then go!' Paul snapped.

Sonia looked at Elise with some concern. She had had a busy day and her visit to Dr Mathoux had given her emotional pressure.

'May I make a suggestion?' she asked tentatively.

'It has nothing to do with you!' Paul snapped again.

'Let her speak,' Edouard intervened.

'She is free of emotional ties and can look at it with unprejudiced eyes.'

Paul raised one eyebrow, as if to question that, but nodded coolly.

'Very well.'

'It obviously affects the whole family but Jerome and Veronique aren't here and it's too late to waken them,' Sonia began nervously. 'Why don't you sleep on it? In the morning you will both have a fresh outlook. You will have to decide whether one man's spell of poor time-keeping is worthy of losing the whole of your trained and previously loyal workforce.'

Paul's eyes narrowed as he looked at her and a shiver ran down Sonia's spine. He didn't like her taking that line. She tried to keep her face impassive as she returned his stare. Then, with a shrug, he capitulated.

'As you say, things will look better in the morning. At least the men will also have had time to reflect on their action and will be ready to compromise.'

'That's fine,' Edouard conceded.

'Tomorrow it is, then.'

With a sigh of relief, Sonia wheeled Elise to her room. They didn't talk much. The incident had taken the shine off the day.

The following day, Paul eventually agreed to meet with the men with an offer to reinstate Allain Mouille, with a proviso that he either worked his full hours or took time off on reduced pay. The men listened in silence as Paul outlined his deal, their faces unsmiling. It was only after Edouard added his pleas for a return to work that the men agreed reluctantly.

At the end of the meeting, Edouard mingled with the men, reaffirming his pledge that neither they nor Allain Mouille would suffer in any way. He moved easily amongst them, greeting them all by name. Jerome did likewise. Paul stood alone, watching his cousin and uncle. His eyes were narrowed but his exact thoughts were unreadable.

Sonia and Elise were watching the proceedings from the rear of the wine-storage room where the meeting was being held. Elise nodded in satisfaction when Edouard's words were heeded.

'I knew they would listen to Edouard,' she whispered. 'He works alongside them, not afraid to get his hands dirty. He knows them.'

Yes, Sonia thought. It's not just that they know him, it's that he knows them. She felt her heart swell with emotion as her eyes followed him around the room, amazed at how much he had come to mean to her in the past few weeks. But then, for a while, he had seemed overshadowed by Paul's more ebullient nature.

She swung her glance to where Paul was standing alone and was startled to find his gaze upon her. He didn't look too pleased. She had the strange thought that he knew exactly what she was thinking, comparing him unfavourably with his cousin. And he didn't like it! He began to thread his way towards her, smiling now, at least, his mouth was. It didn't reach his eyes and she remembered what Elise had said about looking at their eyes. There was no warmth there. She shivered involuntarily.

'Uh, uh,' Elise warned, as Paul came closer.

Sonia tightened her grip on the wheel-chair handles. What now?

'Excuse us for a moment, Elise. I need a word with Sonia.'

Paul's voice was smooth, his expression bland as he led her outside.

'Well, I'm glad all that is over,' he started with a smile. 'We can now get on with other things. Did I mention my forthcoming trip to Paris? It's a business trip, of course, promoting the sale of our wines. I wouldn't leave at his juncture, if it weren't so important but I think I can now safely leave everything here in Edouard's hands.'

Sonia tried to look interested, wondering where all of this was heading.

'I hope your trip is successful, then,' she replied, hoping her voice didn't belie her words. 'Now, I think I'd better go.'

'I want you to come with me.'

She was shocked and stepped backwards.

'Me? Why?'

An amused smile flickered on his lips.

'There is no need to look so alarmed, Sonia. It is beneficial, on these occasions, to have a personal assistant, especially an attractive one.'

He stepped nearer and tilted her chin up towards him.

'You are very beautiful, you know. A beautiful English rose. I'm sure we could manage to enjoy our free time together, very discreetly, of course.'

How dare he! She stiffened and drew away.

'I'm sorry. I have no wish to become involved in any such relationship.'

She sounded prim but she couldn't help it. What had she done to give him the impression that she might be willing to embark on such a relationship? Had she been too friendly, sending out the wrong signals?

'Besides, Elise needs me,' she added.

'My dear Sonia, if that's your objection, I can easily get someone or other to push Elise's wheel-chair around for a few days!'

He seemed to glance past her, then bent his head down towards her. For a moment, she thought he was going to kiss her and tensed her body to step away but he merely smiled close to her face.

'It will give Edouard a chance to win back Corrine. She will, no doubt, run straight back to him when I tell her that she is not, after all, to accompany me to Paris.'

Sonia again felt shock and knew it showed on her face. Paul smiled, as if in amusement.

'Don't set your hopes on Edouard. He still carries a torch for Corrine.'

Sonia's heart plummeted. Edouard and Corrine? She had hoped it was over but she still didn't want to become involved with Paul. She didn't trust him and didn't like his attitude towards other people.

'I'm sorry, but no. If Corrine and Edouard want to resume their relationship then that is up to them.'

'I won't repeat the invitation, neither will I take Edouard's leavings, except for temporary amusement, of course.'

'I am nobody's leavings, as you put it,' Sonia replied. 'And I find this conversation offensive. Now, if you will excuse me.'

She swung around and returned to the wine press with as much dignity as she could muster. Elise was on her way out.

'What did Paul want?' she asked curiously.

'Nothing important. Where is everyone?'

'They have all gone to start work. Did Edouard find you?'

'Edouard? No. How long ago?'

'Just a couple of minutes ago. Not to worry. He will see you later.'

Sonia wondered if he had seen her with Paul and, if so, what had he made of it? Not that it mattered. If he still hoped for a reconciliation with Corrine, there was no point in her hoping he would come to love her. She had better forget him.

With the dispute settled, Sonia and Elise concentrated on making plans for a small party. It could be just the thing to give Elise the optimism she needed to want to become fully mobile again.

'How about a week on Saturday?' Sonia suggested. 'Will that be enough notice?'

'Yes, I think so. How many shall I invite? All my class?'

'If you like. A few may not be able to make it, but that won't matter with a buffet. Elise, what about asking some of your friends to get involved with planning the party? If they feel involved, it will make it easier for you all to resume your friendship. Do you want to try?'

Elise looked petrified.

'Yes, but will you stay with me whilst I ring them all?'

'Of course! Whom will you ring first?'

'Marguerite. We were best friends until I told her not to come anymore. I think I hurt her very much. I wanted to hurt people. It was the only way I could cope with my own hurt.'

'Just tell her you're sorry and see how it goes. Go for it!'

Elise nervously keyed in the number back in her room and listened to the dialling tone. Her face changed colour as the call was answered.

'Marguerite? It's Elise Blaise. Will you talk to me?'

Sonia heard the delighted shriek from the girl on the other end of the line. She stood up, smiling, and waggled her fingers in farewell. Elise was crying but Sonia knew it was best to leave her.

'I'll see you later,' she mouthed. 'I'll be in the kitchen with your mother.'

Veronique was overjoyed at hearing the party plans. Her face lit up as she threw her hands into the air.

'Ooh-la-la! At last! Oh, Sonia! I thank the Lord for the day you came to us. You are so good to my Elise. I think you will get her back on to her feet again, too! Yes?'

Her face suddenly crumpled and tears glistened in her eyes.

'What is it, Veronique? What's the matter? You don't look very well. See, sit down,' Sonia said in concern.

She pulled out a chair and assisted Veronique to sit down, then sank on to her haunches at the side of her and grasped both of Veronique's hands.

'What is it?' she repeated gently.

Veronique was sobbing quietly.

'I don't know, Sonia. I feel so tired I can hardly do my work. I'm not getting enough sleep though I go to bed early enough.'

'Why don't you make an appointment to see the doctor? He'll be able to find out what is the matter with you and give you something to help you.'

'I don't know. What will I tell him? I feel tired? I can't do my work? He'll just tell me to stop moaning and get on with it!'

'No, he won't. Please tell me you'll make an appointment.'

'Maybe. I'll think about it, but let's get this party of Elise's out of the way. Then, maybe, I'll do as you say.'

The next few days were hectic, as the party preparations went ahead. It was good to see the stream of young people calling to see Elise after school and to hear the squeals of girlish laughter and the deeper tones of boys drifting down the passageway. It all served to take Sonia's mind off Paul's strange invitation and the thought of Edouard getting back with Corrine.

Putting aside her personal feelings about her fondness for Edouard, she talked over her worries about Veronique with him and was greatly relieved when Jerome took matters into his own hands and made an appointment for his wife to see the doctor. They didn't pass on their worries to Elise. She was becoming more and more vibrant each day and confided to Sonia that she was going to try to stand on her own before the party. Jeanne, her physiotherapist, was helping her and had high hopes.

The day before the party, Jeanne called at the office as she was leaving.

'Elise wants to see you, Sonia,' she said. 'Have you time to go?'

'Yes, of course. I've nearly finished in here for today anyway.'

Elise was sitting demurely in her wheel-chair, the flush in her cheeks revealing hidden excitement.

'Watch this, Sonia!'

Her face became serious in her effort to concentrate. She placed her hands on the ends of the arm-rests and slowly raised herself out of the chair.

'Elise! You've done it!'

Sonia ran forward to hug the girl. Both of them stood, with tears streaming down their cheeks, not knowing whether to laugh or cry.

'Hello! What's this?'

It was Edouard. He looked from one to the other, not at first realising the cause of the tears.

'It's not Maman, is it?' he asked fearfully.

The girls parted.

'No, Edouard, not Maman.'

'Oh, that's a relief.'

His face suddenly bloomed with incredulity.

'Elise! You're standing!'

He seemed stunned for a moment, as the incredible fact sank in. Then he bounded forward and swung Elise into the air. Elise was looking slightly green when he set her down again but she held out her hand to Sonia, to draw her into the embrace.

'Sonia has helped me, as well as Jeanne,' she said, her eyes bright.

Sonia was conscious of Edouard's arm laid casually across her back and wondered if he was aware of the rapid beat of her heart. She risked a sideways glance and found his dark, smiling eyes disturbingly close. His grip tightened and he leaned closer, his lips brushing against her hair.

'Thank you, Sonia. I knew I had chosen the right girl when I chose you!'

His eyes seemed to say more, but it wasn't the right time.

Elise quickly told them not to tell her parents.

'I want it to be a surprise at my party!'

8

Elise's classmates began to arrive soon after seven on Saturday evening. Paul had arrived home from Paris earlier in the day, exuberant at his success in gaining a number of new wine orders. He joined the others who were busy blowing up balloons, stringing streamers in every available space and extending the dining-room table to its fullest extent.

Edouard organised the setting up of a bar, making sure that the drinks available were a mixture of soft drinks and low alcohol. Elise and her friends had already chosen the music they wanted.

The bustle made it easier for Sonia to accept Paul's involvement in preparing for the party. She felt that he was watching her closely whenever she moved near to Edouard, as if he wanted to gauge their response to each other. Refusing to be intimidated by him, she met his gaze steadily. Even so, she was startled by the satisfied smirk on his face. Well, he was right, really, wasn't he? Although she was now sure that she loved Edouard, and fairly sure he felt something of the same towards her, they hadn't exactly said so to each other.

It was good to see the youngsters enjoying themselves, especially Elise. Her eyes were shining as she greeted each new arrival. A number of them gathered around her wheel-chair, dancing with her as she moved her upper body in time to the music. Thinking of the sullen, unhappy girl whom she had first known, Sonia found it a delight to now see her so happy.

'It is going well,' Edouard murmured in her ear.

His breath felt warm against her skin and the faint fragrance of his aftershave evoked a spiral of butterflies deep within her. She turned to smile at him.

His lips were invitingly close, sending a tingle of longing to her own lips. She raised her eyes, meeting Edouard's. They seemed deep and dark and full of love, she thought joyously. She wasn't sure who moved forward. Maybe they both did. Their lips met and they savoured the taste of each other, moving softly and gently.

Sonia's hands rose to press against Edouard's chest, aware of the rapid beating of his heart. It matched her own and she sighed in happiness. Edouard drew back a little and smiled.

'I have wanted to kiss you for such a long time.'

'Why didn't you?' she breathed.

'Paul seemed to think you preferred him. When I saw him kiss you goodbye before he went to Paris, I assumed he was correct, even though you didn't go with him as he had expected. I was encouraged to notice that you didn't seem to miss him whilst he was away.'

'Paul didn't kiss me goodbye!'

She paused and cast her mind back.

'He said he wanted to talk to me after the meeting and insisted we went outside.'

She frowned, remembering how Paul had leaned forward to whisper in her ear.

'He told me . . . ' she paused again, unsure of what to say.

'Go on,' Edouard encouraged her.

'He said that you wanted to get back with Corrine and it would give you a better chance with her if I went with him.'

She was suddenly uncertain again. Had he wanted Corrine back? Was all this just an interlude with him, carried along by the party atmosphere? She held her breath as she awaited his reply. To her relief, he shook his head.

'Corrine is in the past. We weren't all that serious, otherwise I wouldn't have let her go when Paul crooked his little finger at her!'

He tilted her chin up towards him, his eyes twinkling.

'Do I take it that your response to my kiss means that you feel the same way as I do?'

She smiled happily.

'And what would that be?'

'That I've fallen in love with you.'

She was about to speak when a commotion at the other side of the room drew her attention, and everyone else's.

'Elise! You are standing!'

Veronique dropped the tray of pastries she was carrying in, her face white with shock. She swayed and held out her hand to Jerome.

'Yes, Maman. Stay there! I will walk to you. Sonia! Edouard! Come here!'

Elise was pale but her eyes were alight with determination. Sonia and Edouard hurried over to her, one on each side to support her. Elise carefully grasped hold of their arms and slowly made her way towards her parents.

*   *   *

'What a party!'

It was the following day and Sonia was relieved to find Elise none the worse for her party-trick, although she hadn't felt so optimistic the previous evening when she was helping Veronique to get her ready for bed.

'Are you sure you want to get up this early today?' she asked anxiously.

'Yes. I don't want to slip backwards. I'm going to work really hard at it now. Maman and Papa were pleased, weren't they? I thought Maman was going to faint with shock! Didn't you!'

She chuckled at the memory and Sonia laughed.

'Never mind your mother! I nearly fainted, too, when I realised that you intended to walk!'

Elise grinned at her.

'When I had got to my feet, and everyone was looking at me, it seemed such an anti-climax to just stand there! I decided to give everyone their money's worth!'

'Well, just give us all some warning

next time! I bet your mother didn't sleep a wink last night!'

The smile on Elise's face faded.

'I am worried about her, Sonia. She tries to hide it from me, but I know she isn't well. What is the matter with her?'

'I don't know, but your father has made an appointment for her to see the doctor this afternoon. We should know something then.'

They did — but it wasn't news they wanted to hear.

'He says it is my kidneys,' Veronique told her family. 'He wants me to go into hospital for tests.'

Elise gave a cry.

'Oh, Maman! Did I shock you too much last night? Is it my fault? And I've made life difficult for you since my accident, haven't I?'

Veronique struggled out of her chair and crossed over to her daughter.

'It's not your fault, Elise. It would have happened anyway. It's been coming on for a long time.'

'But I've made extra work for you!'

Elise wailed, looking distraught.

'The extra work only showed up what was already there, love.'

She tried to comfort her daughter.

'And you standing up last night and taking those steps to us made me feel so happy. I can now go into hospital with a lighter heart!'

'I, too, have good news for you, Maman,' Edouard said with a smile.

He stood up and held out his hand towards Sonia. Blushing, she took hold of his hand. Edouard smiled at her and drew her closer to him.

'Sonia and I have realised that we love each other.'

'Oh, wonderful!' Elise cried. 'I knew you would!'

Jerome beamed and rose to shake Edouard's hand and hug Sonia.

'Congratulations, son. You couldn't have made us any happier.'

Veronique held out both her arms and tearfully enveloped Sonia to her.

'Oh, you have made us so happy, Sonia. Welcome to our family.'

The appearance of Paul in the doorway drew everyone's attention. Sonia's stomach somersaulted at the sight of the angry expression in his eyes but, before she had had time to fully take it in, it was gone and he was striding forward with his hand out-stretched to Edouard.

'Congratulations, Edouard. Trust you to take advantage of my absence! Getting your own back for Corrine, eh?'

He thumped Edouard's shoulder playfully, then swung around to Sonia. His dark eyes smouldered and a shiver ran through her.

'You realise you've chosen the wrong one,' he said softly, so that only she could hear. 'Or is it a challenge to me, I wonder.'

'No, to both,' Sonia denied calmly, tossing back her hair.

A faint smile touched his lips.

'We'll see.'

Sonia shivered again, thankful when Jerome spoke out.

'I was just telling the others, Paul. Your aunt has to go into hospital tomorrow to undergo some tests. I trust you can manage without me.'

If there was any sarcasm in his uncle's voice, Paul chose to ignore it.

'What! So soon?' Elise cried, looking alarmed again.

'The sooner the better,' Jerome replied, 'then we can get her on the mend again.'

It was four days before the doctors could give any test result to Jerome, during which time the vines began to flower and the nurturing of the vines with their tender flowers intensified. Jerome arrived home in the late afternoon, his face serious.

'What is it, Papa?' Elise cried.

'I'll put on the kettle,' Sonia offered, sensing that the news wasn't good.

'I have sent young Bernard to tell Edouard and Paul to come. Let's wait until they are here before I start,' Jerome said, sinking wearily on to a chair.

He reached out to squeeze Elise's hand.

'It's all right. We'll pull through,' he comforted her.

As soon as Edouard and Paul were with them, Jerome gave them the doctor's diagnosis, his voice strained and almost breaking.

'Your mother has severe kidney failure,' he said, speaking mainly to Edouard and Elise. 'She is already on dialysis, which should bring immediate results, but it is only a temporary measure. For the best chance of full recovery, she needs a kidney transplant.'

There was a stunned silence, broken by Edouard.

'From one of us?'

Jerome hesitated, as if choosing his words carefully.

'I offered straightaway and had a blood test, but, unfortunately, I am not suitable. It is, of course, possible that a kidney from someone outside the family could be a match, but Veronique has a very rare blood group, which decreases the likelihood of that. Her best chance is one of her children.'

He looked searchingly at Edouard. After a swift glance at Elise, Edouard spoke firmly.

'Then, that means me. No, Elise! I mean it! You have been through enough already.'

He looked at Sonia.

'I have to do it, I want to do it,' he amended. 'She is my mother.'

Sonia crossed over to him and laid her hand on his shoulder.

'I know, and I'm with you all the way.'

'I must tell you that your mother is against it,' Jerome continued. 'She was very upset and forbade me to tell you, but I told her that you deserved to know and deserved the chance to offer a kidney if you wished to do so. But, there is no pressure on you, Edouard. You must talk to the doctor. Although it is now a fairly common procedure, it does carry some risks, and there is always the chance that, at some point of your life, your remaining kidney could be injured or diseased. You must consider all of this, Edouard, with Sonia, too. And if, at any point, you decide against it, there will be no recriminations against you.'

'Hmm! Difficult decision, Edouard!' Paul commented. 'Could you live with the consequences, I wonder.'

Edouard barely acknowledged the words. He spoke directly to Jerome.

'I will do as you say, Papa, but, if all goes well, I will do it!'

Sonia accompanied Edouard to visit Veronique. They had decided that it would be better if Elise were to go the following day with her father, giving Edouard the chance to speak to their mother with Sonia.

As Jerome had said, she was very tearful and adamantly against Edouard donating a kidney.

'You must not do it, Edouard. It's too risky. I forbid you, to even have the test. An appropriate kidney may come my way through the donor scheme.'

'You would accept a kidney from someone who has had to die to give it, but not from me?'

'I would be very grateful to whoever it was but it would be a stranger. I wouldn't know him. I wouldn't worry about the possible risks. Please, Edouard, I couldn't bear it if anything went wrong.'

Tears were pouring down her cheeks.

'Tell him, Sonia. Tell him that he mustn't do this. I'm not worth it!'

Sonia patted her other hand.

'Edouard thinks you are worth it, Veronique, and I agree with him. I would do the same for my mother, or anyone I was close to. It is a privilege to help someone you love.'

She smiled at Edouard, though tears weren't very far away.

'Let him do this for you, Veronique.'

A nurse appeared at the end of the bed.

'Dr Aubrier can speak to you now, Monsieur Blaise. Your mother needs to rest.'

Dr Aubrier greeted them warmly. He carefully outlined the possible dangers to the donor, balanced with the probable benefits to the recipient.

'I do not want you to make up your mind right away,' he told Edouard. 'This is a very emotional time and it is not good to put you under the weight of undue emotional pressure without careful counselling.'

He looked from one to the other.

'What I propose to do today is to take a blood sample and, if that proves to be compatible to your mother's blood group, I will set up a series of counselling sessions for you. How does that sound?'

'Very fair, Doctor Aubrier. We'll go along with that, won't we, Sonia?'

'Yes.'

She clung to his hand, thankful that they had admitted their love for one another before the crisis arose. Less than a week ago, Edouard would have been facing this alone.

They didn't drive straight back

home. Edouard parked the car and they talked, sharing childhood memories, laughed, kissed, putting aside for an hour or so, the momentous decision that would soon confront them.

Sonia took the call from the hospital the following day, whilst Jerome and Elise were visiting Veronique. She went to tell Edouard.

'Dr Aubrier wants to see you as soon as it's convenient, Edouard. His secretary wouldn't say anything further. What do you think it is? Yes or no?'

Edouard wrapped his arms around her.

'I don't know, Sonia, but, for my mother's sake, I hope it is yes.'

Dr Aubrier faced them seriously across his desk when they arrived at the hospital.

'Monsieur Blaise, it isn't often I find myself in this type of situation and I am in a dilemma. I don't know all of your family history, or what demons I might unleash.'

Edouard frowned.

'I don't follow you, Doctor Aubrier. All I am here to learn is whether or not I am a suitable donor of a kidney to my mother. Am I suitable?'

Sonia found she was holding her breath and digging her nails into Edouard's hand. Dr Aubrier inclined his head.

'The answer to that question is simple, Monsieur Blaise. No, you are not.'

His eyes gazed steadily at Edouard, carefully monitoring his reaction. Sonia felt her breath slip out silently. Was it with relief at Dr Aubrier's answer? To be honest, she was relieved, for Edouard. But that didn't help Veronique.

'So, what now?' she asked.

Dr Aubrier rested his elbows on the table, his fingertips touching.

'Wait a minute, Sonia,' Edouard said. 'There's more to this, isn't there, Doctor Aubrier? What was all that preamble about? Why am I not suitable? Have I got the same blood group as my father? Is that why I'm not suitable?'

'It is never quite that simple. Blood groups mix and mingle. Even full brothers and sisters can have different blood groups and different again from the parents. However, there is always some point of contact. Why didn't you tell me that you are not the birth-child of Madame Blaise?'

9

'What?' Edouard exclaimed in amazement, rising from his seat, his face white.

Sonia reached up and took hold of his hand, at the same time looking at Dr Aubrier.

'There must be some mistake,' she said to him. 'Edouard is Veronique's child. Why, he looks so like his father, he has to be their child!'

'Please, sit down, Monsieur Blaise, mademoiselle,' Dr Aubrier requested. 'I am sorry. I didn't realise that you didn't know. Let me explain. Jerome Blaise, your father, has blood group OB. Madame Blaise has a complex group, CDE. Any child of this couple must have either the O or B from Monsieur Blaise and any component or components from Madame Blaise.'

'And,' Edouard prompted, 'what is my group?'

'Your group, monsieur, is AB. The B could be from your father, Monsieur Blaise, and the A must come from your mother. However there is no A in Madame Blaise's blood.'

'So, what exactly are you saying, Doctor Aubrier?'

Edouard's voice was hostile and Sonia knew he was finding this very hard to believe.

'Maybe the blood sample got mixed up with someone else's,' she suggested hesitantly, looking hopefully at Dr Aubrier.

'Perhaps, but it would be very unusual. However, I will arrange for you to have another test.'

He pressed a button on his desk and his secretary appeared.

'Take Monsieur Blaise to the laboratory for another blood test, Mademoiselle Girard. And do not let the sample out of your sight! Tell the technicians that I want them to deal with it immediately.'

The results were back in half an hour. Dr Aubrier looked at them and then at Edouard. He spread his hands.

'It is exactly the same as before, Monsieur Blaise.'

Edouard's face blanched. He gripped tightly on to Sonia's hand.

'So, let me get this straight, Doctor Aubrier,' he said, visibly trying to maintain his composure. 'I may be the son of my father, Monsieur Blaise, that is, but not the son of my mother, of the woman I have called my mother all my life?'

He shook his head in a dazed fashion.

'Then whose son am I? Am I adopted? Is that what you are saying?'

Dr Aubrier spread his hands.

'I don't know. Only your parents know the answer to that. Very often, couples who cannot have a child of their own either adopt a child or make use of the various means of assistance to have a child. Whatever they do, it is because of their great longing to have a child and the love they give to the child is as great as if the child were their own.'

Edouard nodded.

'I know. I have never doubted their love but . . . '

He stood up, taking hold of Sonia's hand once more.

'I need time to sort this out, Doctor Aubrier. I am sure you understand.'

'Of course! All I ask is that you do not storm in to see your mother. She is really quite poorly and I do not want her to be upset at this stage. Agreed?'

'Yes.'

Still feeling dazed, Edouard and Sonia shook Dr Aubrier's hand and left his office. Edouard strode down the corridor.

'Edouard! You aren't going to see your mother, are you?' Sonia asked.

'No! The one with the answers will be my father! Do you realise, he probably had an affair and my mother accepted his . . . his love child!'

They caught up with Jerome back at home. He, Elise and Paul were halfway through an early evening meal, prior to Jerome returning to visit Veronique that evening. Edouard dived straight in.

'Why didn't you tell me, Papa? Did you think I wouldn't love Maman, your wife, that is? Or that I wouldn't respect you? I would have respected you far more than I do right now!'

All three raised startled eyes to him. Jerome scraped back his chair and stood up.

'I don't know what you are talking about, Edouard! What has happened? Have you seen Dr Aubrier? What did he say?'

'What do you think he said? That, yes, I was an ideal match for this woman who isn't my real mother?'

'What?'

'Mon dieu!'

This was from Paul, who had suddenly realised where the conversation was going. His eyes gleamed in anticipation. Edouard ignored him. His

169

eyes were locked with Jerome's. Jerome glared back at him.

'I repeat, I don't know what you are talking about, Edouard. Of course your mother is your mother! Who else would she be?'

'My blood group shows that I cannot be Maman's birth child, whatever she became to me afterwards. So, whose child was I? And why was I never told?'

'This is ridiculous, Edouard. What exactly are you suggesting? You have only to look into the mirror to know that you are our son.'

'That you are my father isn't in doubt. The question is, who is really my mother?'

Jerome threw up his hands in impatience.

'It is madness! I was there when your mother went into labour and I took her to the hospital. I admit I wasn't there when you were born, but I visited the hospital a few hours later. There must be some mistake.'

'I think he is suggesting that you had

been a naughty boy, Uncle Jerome,' Paul suggested, grinning broadly. 'How did you manage the changeover? Did you bribe the nurses? And what became of Aunt Veronique's child? To think I have underestimated you, all these years!'

'Stay out of this, Paul! You are talking rubbish!' Jerome snapped.

He turned back to Edouard.

'And so are you, Edouard! I have never looked at another woman besides your mother! I don't know what Dr Aubrier has said to you, but I am going to find out! I shall insist that they do another blood test. They've probably mixed it up with someone else's!'

'We have already done that, Papa. It was exactly the same.'

Nevertheless, Jerome strode out of the room and they could hear his voice speaking sharply on the telephone. Elise tried to get out of her wheel-chair to go to Edouard but he crossed over to her and bent to hug her.

'I am still your sister, Edouard, whatever happens!' she assured him.

'I know. Don't worry. It has all been a bit of a shock and I am still reeling. Quite suddenly, I don't know who I am.'

'And you're still my cousin,' Paul said, half-mockingly. 'What a turn-up, eh? And I thought I was the one who didn't know my parents! They've certainly kept that secret close to their hearts all these years! No wonder Aunt Veronique didn't want you to offer her your kidney. She knew it would reveal their long-hidden secret!'

'There's more to it than that,' Sonia mused quietly. 'Jerome seemed to be as shocked as we were.'

They all fell silent again as Jerome returned. He was still very agitated.

'I am going to the hospital to sort this out. You had better come, too, Edouard.'

'I want to come as well,' Elise insisted. 'Maman will need me, and so will Edouard.'

After a slight hesitation, Jerome agreed.

'Very well, but I don't want any upset. Whatever has happened, your mother needs to be kept calm.'

'Do you mind if I come as well?' Paul asked. 'After all, I am family.'

Sonia glanced at him sharply, expecting to see a mocking expression on his face but was pleased to see only concern there. She smiled encouragingly at him, aware that, like him, she, too, was outside the close family circle, allowed in only by their permission.

Jerome insisted that he went to speak to Veronique alone first and the other four agreed. They waited in silence. When Jerome appeared in the doorway of the private room where Veronique was still undergoing her dialysis treatment, his face portrayed very little of whatever had gone on between him and his wife.

Sonia sensed that he was in total shock, but couldn't determine exactly what he was feeling. She looked up anxiously at Edouard but his face, too, was impassive. He managed to give a tight smile in response to her squeeze on his hand but she could tell he was very tense. She couldn't imagine what it must be like to suddenly discover that the woman you had thought to be your mother, in fact, wasn't. No matter how much you had felt loved and wanted, it would still be a shock.

Who was his mother? What had become of her? Was she dead? Edouard had stood up, pulling her with him, and they were following Elise into the small room. Paul unwound his long legs and sauntered after them, keeping his thoughts very much to himself.

Veronique was very pale and very distressed. It was obvious to them all that she had been crying and Sonia wondered if it were wise to have them all in the room together. Jerome sank down on to a chair at the side of the bed, indicating to them all to do likewise. He took hold of Veronique's hand but his eyes were on Edouard.

'I don't know where to start,' he said flatly, looking at them all. 'I am afraid that you are all in for a shock.'

Veronique began to cry again. She buried her face in her hands.

'I am so sorry, Edouard! I am so sorry! I didn't think of the consequences! I just did it. It didn't seem so dreadful. You were both new-born babies. Your identity tags hadn't been put on and you looked so alike. Who would ever know, I thought?'

The blood drained from Edouard's face as he leaned forward.

'What are you saying?'

Alarm was beginning to show in Paul's face, too. His body tensed as he also leaned forward, disbelief spreading across his face. Veronique looked from one to the other, her fingers spread across her mouth.

'I changed you two boys over. It didn't seem fair. Jerome was the younger twin and now, his son, Paul, was born first but still wouldn't inherit!

I wanted my son . . . our son . . . to inherit.'

Her voice dropped to a whisper.

'It was very wrong of me. I know that now. It has torn me apart, loving my son, who was not my son.'

She held out her hand towards Paul, but he ignored it, staring at her with an ashen face. She turned back to Edouard and burst into tears again, turning desperately to Jerome, burying her face into his chest.

'Maman!' Elise cried, not believing what she had heard.

Sonia's main concern was for Edouard. How was he taking it, now knowing that Veronique was his aunt, not his mother, and that, by her action, she had disinherited him. Edouard and Paul were both standing now, facing each other across the bed. Both were shocked, but Paul's face portrayed scorn and anger.

'I don't believe you!' he said harshly. 'This is some ploy to gain control of the business.'

He pointed his right hand accusingly at Veronique.

'You are not my mother! I have no mother! My mother is dead! Do you know how often I cried for my mother when I was a child? But you were Edouard's mother, not mine! I was on my own and I will stay on my own!'

He backed towards the door as he spoke, his hand still shaking towards Veronique and Jerome.

'And you!'

He swung his threatening hand to point it at Edouard.

'You will never take over from me!'

Edouard moved towards Paul.

'We need to talk it through, Paul. If what Maman says is true, we need to come to some sort of settlement and, if you are her true son, do you realise you may be the perfect match for a kidney?'

'You must be joking!' Paul said scathingly. 'She is not my mother and she'll get nothing from me! I suggest you get yourselves a good solicitor. You are going to need one!'

While the others still stared at him in shock, he whisked open the door and stormed out.

★   ★   ★

They saw nothing more of Paul for the next few days. It gave the rest of the family the opportunity to discuss and come to terms with Veronique's dramatic revelation. Not that that was easy, Sonia reflected. It had shattered every relationship in the family except hers and Edouard's. Edouard was no longer a son and a brother but a nephew and cousin. He was now the one who didn't know his parents and told Sonia that he felt he didn't know himself any more.

'I need to talk to Paul,' he said. 'We've got to come to some arrangement. It wasn't his fault that he's been brought up to believe that he was me.'

He drew Sonia close.

'Would you mind if I suggest that we split it all fifty-fifty? Paul could concentrate on the wine side of the

178

business and I could develop the distillery. It would be what I wanted to do anyway, except Paul wouldn't agree. Now, it could be the way to heal everything.'

'It's more than generous of you but just what I expected of you. I hope Paul agrees. Have you no idea where he has gone?'

'No. I'll get in touch with his solicitor. I'm sure he'll be in touch when he's had time to come to terms with everything. In the meantime, we'll keep it all within the family. There's a lot of work to be done. Now that the vines have flowered, we know when the harvest will start. I'm going to check the storage vats today. Allain Mouille would have done it normally, but it's one of the things that got overlooked while he's been on leave of absence. It will help to take my mind off things for a while. What are you planning today?'

'Elise wants me to take her shopping. Is it all right if we use the hatchback? We'll take the collapsible wheel-chair.

She will need it in town.'

'Yes. Have a good time. I'll see you at lunchtime.'

It was a relief to get away from the farm for a few hours. Although Edouard and Jerome had talked and assured each other that their changed status by no means changed their feelings for each other, there was still a degree of tension in the air. Edouard had admitted to her that he felt Veronique had betrayed him but knew that she did love him dearly. As each day passed, he found it easier to understand her impetuous action all these years ago and had already told her that he forgave her.

She knew that Paul wouldn't find it quite as easy to forgive Veronique. She wasn't sure which aspect would hurt him the more — Veronique pretending that he was her nephew instead of her son to enable him to inherit the family business or that she had now admitted her deceit and denied him his position as head of the family.

Lost in her thoughts, she was suddenly brought back to the present by a squeal from Elise.

'That was Paul! I'm sure it was!'

She turned round, straining to see the red sports car that was speeding away in the direction of the farm.

'Are you sure?'

'Yes! Yes! Stop, Sonia! We must go back!'

Sonia pulled over as soon as she could and switched off the engine.

'Let's just think it through, Elise. Suppose it was Paul and that he's going home, will he want to see us all? He might prefer to see just Edouard and Jerome at first. They have a great deal of adjustments to make. He's not going to find any of it easy.'

'That's the point! You don't know him as well as I do, Sonia. He can be very vindictive. He won't just accept this quietly. He'll be going back in there with all guns blazing!'

Sonia knew that Elise was right.

'All right. Let's go!'

She had to drive a few kilometres before she found a place suitable for turning round but they were soon on their way back home. She knew she wouldn't be able to catch up with Paul, not the way Paul drove along these twisting roads, so she kept safely within her own capabilities. As they turned into the long, private drive, she reckoned they could be ten to fifteen minutes behind Paul.

To their surprise, Paul's car was parked about halfway along the drive. Now, why would he do that? She pulled up and looked around, wondering if Paul had seen Edouard working in the fields and had gone over to talk to him. But, no, Edouard was inspecting the storage vats this morning.

'He's parked here so that no-one will see him arrive,' Elise stated.

Sonia immediately slipped into first gear and accelerated swiftly towards the house. Quite suddenly, she felt alarmed. One glance at Elise showed that she wasn't alone in her anxiety. She pulled up sharply in the yard and switched off the engine.

'Elise! You must get yourself out. I want to find Edouard.'

She leaped out of the car and ran across the cobbied yard into the fermenting house. Once inside, she stopped abruptly. The two men were on the high gantry around the top of the large concrete fermenting tanks. One of them, Edouard, she hoped, was holding on to part of the gantry framework with one hand, struggling with this other hand to restrain Paul, who seemed to be trying to throw him over the rail. Hooking a foot through Edouard's legs, Paul pulled Edouard off balance. Edouard managed to keep hold of the metal bar, though he staggered slightly.

Sonia rushed forward.

'Stop it, Paul! Stop! What are you doing?' she screamed.

Paul swung round, his attention diverted. At the same moment, Elise appeared in the doorway.

'Paul!'

Her voice made him swing his glance back to the door and then, in slow motion, it seemed to Sonia, he fell. Sonia froze then she found herself kneeling at Paul's side, feeling for his pulse.

'He's still alive! Stay there, Elise. I'll get back to you. I'm going to phone for an ambulance.'

Aware that Edouard was safely descending the ladder, she rushed over to the house, made the call, and ran back. Edouard had covered Paul with a horse blanket while three of the stable boys hovered uncertainly. She tossed her car keys to one of them.

'Get the wheel-chair out of the boot, Marc. Elise needs to sit down.'

'And you, Pierre, go and watch out for the ambulance!' Edouard ordered. 'Bernard, find my father. Tell him to come here immediately.'

He stood up and held out his arms to Sonia. She slipped into them, hugging him tightly. She shuddered. For some dreadful moments, she had feared that both the young men would fall. She had nearly lost him! It was bad enough as it was! She looked down at Paul. His face was white. Edouard's glance followed hers.

'He was trying to kill me, Sonia!' he said in shocked tones.

'I know. How is he?' she whispered.

'Still alive, just! I daren't move him. Hold on! He's trying to say something.'

He dropped down to Paul's side and put his ear close to Paul's mouth. There was a strange rattling sound and, when Edouard stood up again, Sonia knew that Paul had died.

'Did you manage to catch what he said?' she asked.

Edouard nodded.

'He said, 'Let her have it.''

★ ★ ★

It was mid-July when Veronique was discharged from the hospital. She came home to a subdued family. They had talked through the various possibilities of action to take and had decided to leave matters as they were. Since Paul was unmarried and had no heir, Jerome, as next in line, was now the head of the family business, with Edouard as the manager. He was content to know that the business would become his in years to come.

'It's best, this way,' Edouard said to Sonia. 'I don't think any of us could face the legal minefield if we tried to put things right. Can you bear to marry into such a mixed-up family?'

He drew her close and she snuggled her head against his shoulder.

'I'm marrying you, not your family.'

She smiled, lifting up her head and looking into his eyes.

'And, together, we'll all pull through.'

THE END ✓